JuliScott
Super Sleuth
Book 6

W9-BNF-792

Saturday Scare

Colleen L. Reece

*Enjoy!
Colleen
Reece*

BARBOUR
PUBLISHING, INC.
Uhrichsville, Ohio

Saturday
Scare

Published by Barbour Publishing, Inc.
P.O. Box 719
Uhrichsville, Ohio 44683
http://www.barbourbooks.com

 Member of the
Evangelical Christian
Publishers Association

CHAPTER 1

"Earth to Juli. Earth to Juli. Do you read me?" Shannon asked in a booming voice. She added, in her own Irish accent, "Mercy me, you're a gazillion miles away," spoiling her imitation of TV space shows.

Sixteen-year-old Juli Scott shook her head so hard, she nearly dislodged the clip holding her blondish-brown hair back from her face. "Wrong. I'm walking home from the bus stop in Bellingham, Washington with my spacey friend." She fixed a stern blue gaze on Shannon's merry face. "By the way, haven't I told you a gazillion times not to exaggerate?"

"At least," Shannon solemnly agreed before erupting into a contagious laugh that made Juli smile in spite of herself. Shannon's blue-gray eyes shone, and a bright gold maple leaf drifted down and parked on her short, crow-black hair.

"If I didn't know you so well, I'd say you had a halo," Juli teased. She twitched the leaf off and scuffed through the piles of leaves that blanketed the sidewalk. She sniffed the tang of wood smoke that mingled with a faintly salt breeze coming in off Bellingham Bay. "I love autumn days like this." She looked up at intense blue speckled with puffy white clouds which moved at a snail's pace across the sky. "All the red and yellow and orange leaves make everything colorful and terrific. There ought to be a special word to describe it."

"Colorific," Shannon prompted. Hands on her hips, elbows akimbo, she did an impromptu Irish jig on the sidewalk, to the amusement of those in a passing car who laughed and cheered.

Juli stared suspiciously. "Is that really a word, or are you making it up?"

Shannon stopped her whirling-dervish act and looked hurt. "Would I do that?"

"Don't give me that wounded look. And you've been in America long enough to lose your accent, except when you're upset or acting crazy," Juli reminded.

"Yes, mother." Mischief sparkled in Shannon's eyes. She folded her hands like a good little girl in an old-fashioned storybook. "Ever since the beginning of our sophomore year, twelve months and some odd weeks ago, to be exact."

"You're right about the odd weeks," Juli retorted. "One week around you is odder than anyone needs! Give. Is 'colorific' a word or a Rileyism?"

Shannon clasped her hands and smirked. "I'll never tell. You can be for lookin' it up when we get to your house." She placed her hands back on her hips and gave

Juli a mock glare. "And don't be for makin' fun of the way I talk. My quotations always make sense, don't they?"

"*Mis*quotations is more like it. The worst thing is, you have everyone else doing it. Including me." Juli felt embarrassment redden her face until it matched the flaming sumac shrub next to the sidewalk. "When Dave Gilmore said he could beat me at tennis, I said 'in your nightmares,' instead of 'in your dreams'!"

Shannon doubled over laughing. "I wish I'd been there."

"I'm glad you weren't." Juli's mouth turned down. "You're a bad influence, getting everything backward the way you do. I used to talk like a *normal* person."

"Whatever that is." Shannon dismissed the comment with an airy wave of her hand. They good-naturedly argued the rest of the way to Juli's pale yellow ranch-style house with white shutters, where Shannon felt as much at home as Juli. Colored flowers that matched the leaf piles on the emerald lawn spilled from window boxes and lined the walk from the gate to the front porch. The solid door stood open to the warm autumn day, and the top half of the locked storm door wore only a screen to let in fresh air.

Juli sighed. Soon they'd put the glass back in. Bellingham winters brought snow, ice, and cold weather. Her sigh gave way to anticipation. Winter also brought skiing and sledding. She and Shannon, along with the rest of their friends, loved both. "Mom?" she called. "Let us in, will you, please?"

An older edition of Juli hurried to unlock the door.

Mom's cheeks matched her scarlet sweatshirt that bore the words "Homemaker First Class"—the shirt was a favorite choice when she came home from teaching first grade weekday mornings. "Thank God I'm able to team teach," she'd said many times. "Working half-days and having afternoons off gives me the best of both worlds."

"Not to mention what it does for your devoted husband and darling daughter," her tall, dark-haired Washington State Police officer husband, Gary, often added. "Knowing I can come home to your cooking makes my day."

"Only my cooking? Thanks a lot." Anne's pretense at being offended never quite succeeded.

Juli always felt warm all over when Dad's gray eyes would twinkle and he'd say to Mom, "If you only cooked TV dinners, I'd still be eager and happy to come home," and then he'd drop a quick kiss on her nose.

Now Mom welcomed the girls with impartial hugs. "Hi, daughter and second daughter. Come on out to the kitchen. I have the chili on high. Dad will be here any minute and we need to eat early. There's a meeting at church tonight."

Juli and Shannon followed her and the scent of spices and baking bread through the pale green dining room— the table was set with four places—to the blue-and-white, country-look kitchen. "Is the extra plate for me?" Shannon asked hopefully. "Dad has to work late at the bank, so I'm available." She grinned.

"What do you think?" Mom teased.

"She knows you'd never turn down hot rolls and chili," Juli put in. It felt so good not to have to come home to an empty house and start dinner the way she'd had to when Dad was gone so long and Mom had to work full-time. *Thank You, God,* she silently prayed. *You've brought us through so much.*

"What can we do to help?" Shannon asked as she washed her hands at the sink.

"Get the tossed salad and chilled salad plates from the fridge. And pour ice water." Mom deftly slid a pan of yeast rolls from the oven.

Juli grabbed her stomach. "This is torture! When did you say Dad is coming? I'm starving."

"So am I," her father answered, amusement in his voice, before giving her a hug. "How are my girls?" Gary Scott patted Shannon's shoulder and kissed Mom.

"Fine," they answered in unison.

The conversation all through dinner was lively, but at times Juli found her attention wandering. Anyone looking into their home tonight who didn't know all the facts would label the Scotts a perfect family. Yet they had faced tragedy, danger, threats, and separation that had turned their world upside down and had threatened to destroy them. Again Juli gave silent thanks. God had been with Juli, her family, and her friends every step of the way. If He hadn't. . .she shuddered. She was no coward, but even imagining what might have happened without the love and protection of their heavenly Father sent icy inch-worms looping up and down her spine.

Shannon called her father at the bank and asked him to pick her up at Juli's house after his meeting. The people who had harassed the girls and others of the senior high church youth group were in custody or serving prison terms, but Shannon still disliked being home alone. They volunteered for kitchen cleanup, shooed Gary and Anne off to their meeting, and headed for the wood-paneled living room that faced the street.

Juli closed the drapes against the early night and looked longingly at the fireplace insert. "No point in building a fire, I guess. The house is pretty cozy from Mom's baking." She kicked off her shoes, curled up on one end of the comfortable couch, and locked her hands behind her head.

Shannon followed suit. "It feels so peaceful. Know what? Today is like when we first met. Only better, because your dad is home."

"I know. Things are great." Juli ticked off items on her fingers. "No more being trailed. No more threatening notes. Or vandalism. Everything's fine with Dave." She felt her heart beat a little faster at the thought of her brown-haired basketball-playing boyfriend. "And Ted."

The look on Shannon's face showed that her heartbeat had quickened, too, at mention of Ted Hilton, another ballplayer and her special friend. To Juli's surprise, the Irish girl looked far more serious than the conversation. "Ted is worried about what's happening to Amy. You know how close twins are. I'm worried, too."

"So am I." Juli snuggled deeper into the couch cushions and pictured the petite blonde cheerleader. "Ever since she and Carlos started liking each other, Amy Hilton has been a different person—more like Ted. It isn't fair! Just when she stops being a jerk, the popular crowd snubs her. I hope she can handle it. The whole thing is dumb." She pounded the arm of the couch. "Why should Carlos Ramirez get hassled just because he's the son of migrant workers? He's one of the nicest guys around. Hardworking, too, or the Thompsons wouldn't have invited him to live with them and go to school this year."

"Our youth leaders know what prejudice is like," Shannon pointed out. "Remember when Kareem shared how his whole family was killed in a tribal war in Africa? If missionaries hadn't adopted him and brought him to the United States, who knows what might have happened to him?"

Juli soberly added, "America is still a long way from overcoming prejudice. I wonder how God feels when He sees the way people treat those like Carlos and the Thompsons, who love and serve Him? All they want is to be left alone."

"Racial or any kind of hatred affects everyone," Shannon whispered. Her eyes looked enormous. "I'd love to take you to Ireland, but I wonder. Do we really want to visit a place where people kill each other because of religion?"

The pain in her face told how hard it was for Shannon to think of the turmoil and killing in her homeland. "We can't do anything about the situation in Ireland, but maybe we can do something right here in Bellingham," Juli slowly said.

"What?" Shannon wanted to know. "I can't see us picketing the school and shouting 'Down with prejudice' or 'Help stamp out hatred.' "

"I don't know," Juli confessed. "It just seems some-one should do something for all the Carloses and Kareems and all the others who are treated so awful."

A thoughtful expression crossed Shannon's face. "Remember the old saying about not knowing people, so we dislike them?"

"It's the other way around," Juli corrected. "We don't like people because we don't know them."

"Whatever." Shannon impatiently brushed the comment aside. "You know how our principal is always bragging about Hillcrest being so multicultural. Why not ask him if we can have a special assembly recognizing our diversity? Maybe even a talent show, with different people performing something that represents their heritage." Her idea grew like Jack's magic beans. "What if we held it at night and sold tickets to parents and friends? It would be a great junior class fund-raiser, as well as making the kids more aware that different can be good."

Juli untangled her legs and got up from the couch. "This calls for a ways and means committee."

"Meaning you're going to call Dave and Ted," Shannon translated.

"Bingo." Juli stopped on her way to the phone and said, "In spite of your Rileyisms, I have hope for you. Sometimes you show signs of absolute genius."

"Think nothing of it," Shannon modestly told her. "Of course I won't object if you're for callin' me Dr. Einstein."

"In your nightmares," Juli called over her shoulder. She followed it with a laugh before ignoring Shannon's groan and dialing.

By the time the girls set out juice and cookies, Dave and Ted arrived. Both looked scrubbed and clean-cut, rather than handsome. "You rang?" Ted said in an affected imitation of the family butler who inevitably appeared in many old black and white movies. Dave just cocked an eyebrow at Juli and glued his imploring gaze on the cookies.

She took the hint, motioned the boys to chairs, and passed the plate.

"Thanks. It's been at least an hour since dinner." Dave made short work of one and reached for a second, although cookies at the Scott house definitely leaned toward being king-size. "So. What's up?"

"We are. Up in the sky about the way some people treat other people because of their backgrounds," Shannon exploded.

"Excuse me?" Dave stared, the second cookie half-way to his mouth.

Ted let out a whoop of laughter. "Don't you mean 'up in the air'?"

"Air. Sky. What's the difference? It's just plain wrong," Shannon insisted.

His laughing stopped. "I'll buy that. Amy came home in tears today. Seems she's getting pressure to either dump Carlos or consider her cheerleading days at good old Hillcrest history."

Juli choked on a crumb and indignation. When she stopped coughing she burst out, "No way! The student body elected Amy. What are the snobs going to do, get kids to sign a petition and recall her?"

Admiration shone in Ted's face. "That's what she told them. I'm beginning to see a different side to my twin sister. I didn't know she had it in her."

"How do your folks feel about all this?" Shannon asked.

Ted looked worried. "I think they're struggling. They like Carlos but hate to see Amy lose everything she's worked so hard to achieve." He shifted in his chair. Juli suspected he felt uncomfortable. "Dad and Mom are also concerned about how much Amy likes Carlos. She's only sixteen. Mom caught her looking at a bride's catalog. She got this crazy idea Amy may do something stupid if the kids at school push her too hard." He tried to grin but it came out sickly. "Don't let on I said anything. I'm not supposed to know about it."

His warning barely registered. "You mean stupid as in elope?" Juli squeaked.

"I told you it was a crazy idea."

"You're the one who's being stupid," Dave bluntly told his best friend. "Even if Amy didn't have any better sense than to pull off such a stunt, which she *does*, Carlos wouldn't go for it in a million years!"

"I'm not so sure," Ted mumbled. "He thinks my sister's pretty special."

"We think Juli and Shannon are pretty special, too, but we aren't hauling ladders to their windows for an old-fashioned elopement, are we?"

Dave's challenge brought back the old Ted. "No," he drawled. "Although once when she was out of it, Shannon asked me to run away with her."

Red flags came to her cheeks. " 'Tis good ye refused! I'd be givin' ye the back of me arm, if ye took advantage of me bein' drugged by wicked folk."

Juli didn't dare laugh. She did say, "That's the back of your hand, not arm."

"Are we going to discuss my idea? Dad will be here soon."

"You bet we are!" Juli avoided looking at Dave. Shannon was in no mood to have her best friend burst into laughter. Juli knew one look at Dave's broadly grinning face could prove fatal to her already shaky self-control.

CHAPTER 2

"Whatever you do, don't call our principal 'Mr. Smiles,' "
Juli hissed just before she and Shannon reached the office
the next morning before school started.

Shannon grunted. "You honestly think Mr. S.—short
for Samuel—Miles doesn't know every student at
Hillcrest calls him that?"

"But not to his face," Juli insisted, although she secretly
agreed with Shannon. The longtime principal kept all
eight fingers and both thumbs on the pulse of Hillcrest
High. His high expectations, strong discipline, and car-
ing vigilance made Hillcrest an acknowledged leader in
Whatcom County. Woe to those who thought they could
get away with guns or drugs at Mr. Smiles's school!

The round-faced man whose genial countenance
hid a computer-sharp brain greeted the girls with,
"Good morning, Shannon. Julianne. What can I do for
you?" His broad smile made his nickname more appropriate than ever.

Call me Juli, for starters, she wanted to say. No matter how often she reminded Mr. Smiles, the next time he saw her, he used her full name. She didn't mind in the privacy of his office, just in the halls. She cringed every time he boomed "Julianne," knowing mocking echoes from fellow students would follow.

Shannon's eyes looked more blue than gray above her soft blue sweater. While Juli was still waffling about correcting the Julianne, Shannon said, "We wanted to ask you about a possible junior class project."

"Have you discussed it with your class advisor?" Mr. Smiles asked.

Shannon shook her dark head. "It involves the community as well as the school." In her eagerness to impress the principal, she lapsed into brogue. "We would like to be for sponsorin' a talent show," she announced.

"Not the ordinary kind," Juli put in. She bit her tongue. Shannon had thought up the plan. She should be the one to introduce it.

The principal chuckled. "A talent show is a talent show, isn't it? What do you have in mind to make it extraordinary?"

"We want to be for askin' all those who participate to do somethin' that represents their ethnic backgrounds," Shannon explained.

"Is this just about making money for your class?" Mr. Smiles's keen gaze bored into Shannon, then fixed itself on Juli.

Juli took a deep breath. How could she tell the principal some of the school leaders were guilty of racial prejudice and harassment? The thought of Amy crying strengthened her. She could get the point across without mentioning names.

Before she could speak, Shannon said in a small voice, "Mr. S—uh, Miles, Hillcrest is multicultural, but we really aren't for bein' integrated."

"Have you been made to feel unwelcome here?" he barked.

Shannon turned bright red. "Oh, no." She blinked long, dark lashes that never needed mascara. "Mercy me! I've been treated fine. I love it here."

"That's because of your Rileyisms," Juli teased, hoping to remove the thundercloud spreading over Mr. Smiles's face.

Shannon shot her an exasperated glance. "It's just that certain kids are for bein' left out when the feathered birds stick together in a flock, and—"

Her latest Rileyism did what Juli's comment had failed to accomplish. Mr. Smiles burst into laughter. "Don't you mean birds of a feather flock together?"

She grinned good-naturedly. "For certain. Sorry I've been blatherin' on."

The principal wiped his eyes. "Don't be, Shannon. I've noticed the cliques and been pondering what to do about them. I can't very well force students to hang out with other students. Your idea of helping develop awareness and appreciation for other cultures is excellent." He relaxed and fitted the tips of his fingers together, a gesture Juli had seen too many times to count.

"There is one drawback," he said after a moment.

Juli's heart sank. She glanced at Shannon, whose lower lip now drooped. Juli burst out, "I thought you liked the idea."

"I do, Julianne," Mr. Smiles quietly said. "I also feel it's too good an opportunity to limit it to a class project. Doing so means only Hillcrest students and their parents or friends will benefit. I'd like to see your plan expanded. How about my approaching the principal at Cove High and asking if he wants his school to participate? It could more than double the audience."

"Yes!" Juli's hands shot into the air.

"Shannon? I take it this was your idea?"

"It's grrrand!" she exclaimed, her Irish accent more pronounced than ever.

Juli's mind raced like cars on a track. "If the Cove principal says yes, Ashley Peterson and I can write about it in our weekly column," she offered. "Kids all over Whatcom County are reading it, calling and writing to us." She thought of the bad feeling between Ashley and her before the two girls tied in the newspaper's essay contest and became coauthors of the young adult column. A frank discussion of their feelings brought mutual respect and growing acceptance. Juli secretly made a face. The trouble between her and Ashley was an excellent example of judging and not liking someone because she didn't know her.

Leave it to Shannon to make one more blunder before their interview with Mr. Smiles ended! He asked them to stay while he phoned the principal at Cove. He explained the idea in simple turns, not glossing over the main reason for the show, and ending with, "Our schools can split the profits after we take out expenses. What do you say? There's a lot more at stake here than money."

The girls tensely waited on the edge of their chairs. Mr. Smiles listened and nodded for what seemed like forever to the girls. He said "Uh-huh" a couple of times before cradling the phone and turning his full moon face toward them. "I believe the word you use for a successful venture is 'bingo.' Right?"

"Right," they chorused. The warning bell rang. They scrambled to their feet and grabbed their books. "Thanks," Juli said.

Shannon innocently added, "Oh, yes. You're a dar—"

"Come on or we'll be late," Juli interrupted. One of Shannon's expressions when excited was to call someone a darling man. Juli repeatedly told her it might be fine for Ireland but was definitely uncool in Bellingham. Still, her friend occasionally slipped and used the expression. Juli didn't know how Mr. Smiles would react to such a comment!

"I'll notify the teachers and call an all-school assembly for the last half of last period," the principal promised, walking them to the door. "If you don't make it to class on time, come back and get a late pass from me." He eagerly rubbed his hands together, showing the girls how excited he was about the idea.

Just before school ended, the Hillcrest principal strode across the platform of the large assembly room, again rubbing his hands. "This morning two students approached me with a dynamite idea. They asked me to withhold their names."

Juli tried to look innocent, hating the red tide she felt rising from the collar of her white shirt. She sneaked a look at Shannon. She wasn't doing so well, either. A rich blush had colored her smooth skin.

"Methinks everyone will know who those students are if you and Shannon don't stop blushing," Dave Gilmore whispered in Juli's ear. "Fine thing. How do you expect to remain a super sleuth and senior partner in Scott and Gilmore, P.I.s—famous private investigators—if you can't control your expression?"

The word "methinks" took Juli back to a snowy evening months earlier, when Dave had teased her by quoting their Honors writing teacher, Mrs. Sorenson. Juli's lips twitched and she whispered back, "Shh. God gave us two ears and only one mouth. That means we're supposed to listen twice as much as we talk."

Dave muffled his laugh into a loud cough that subsided after several students sent withering glances their way.

As Mr. Smiles talked, the student body went from showing mild interest to excited anticipation. Few could resist the principal's contagious enthusiasm. In addition, he made an announcement that surprised even Juli and Shannon.

"Since originally contacting the principal at Cove, I've been on the phone with him a couple of more times. We agreed to an incentive, in case some of you aren't wild about getting up in front of people." A buzz rippled through the auditorium.

"So what's the incentive?" a funny-looking but well-liked senior boy called out. "A date with me?" The buzz changed to a roar and catcalls.

When the noise died down, Mr. Smiles announced, "Sorry, nothing that special." He grinned at the boy, who pretended to wipe away tears at the unrestrained groans of relief greeting the principal's announcement.

"There will be first, second, and third place prizes of $50, $35, and $20 cash for the individual or group the judges feel best represents a specific heritage. One thing: If any of you have performed professionally—in other words, for money—please say so when signing up. We want to include you, but the prizes will be restricted to amateurs. There will be more details after we work things out with Cove."

"All right!" The assembly broke up in loud cheering.

"Smart move," Ted applauded when the final bell of the day sounded. He kept his voice low, and Juli was thankful. "For fifty bucks, I'd almost consider getting up there. If I had any talent, that is. Pretty hard to win a talent contest by shooting free throws." He smiled at Shannon. "Did you and Juli know he was going to offer prizes?"

"No." The Irish girl looked a little dazed. "I also didn't know this would be for turnin' into a big deal." She waved at the knots of students who had lingered to discuss the show. If talent matched the early interest, it would be a great event.

"Uh-oh, I just thought of something." Juli broke away from her friends and headed toward Mr. Smiles. The teachers congratulating him walked out of hearing and she asked, "How are we going to make sure the talent is worth the price people have to pay to come see it?" She licked suddenly dry lips. "The whole thing could bomb if just anyone gets up on the stage."

He looked serious. "What do you feel is more important? Presenting a polished show or involving students who otherwise seldom have a chance?"

"Use anyone who wants to be in the show," Shannon said from behind Juli. "The whole idea is to have as many cultures as possible represented."

"Agreed?" Mr. Smiles asked Juli.

"Of course." Her brain threw ideas like corn in a popper. "Why don't we call it a variety show, rather than a talent show? We could put in the advertising that the first part of the evening will be amateurs. If some professionals sign up, they can perform after the prizes have been awarded so no one will feel intimidated."

Mr. Smiles nodded. "Great idea. We'll need a committee for this, using students from both schools. Do you girls want to be on it? How about you two?" he asked Dave and Ted, who had followed Juli and Shannon.

Juli opened her mouth to say yes. A nudge from Shannon silenced her. She admired her friend's sensitivity when she said, "I don't mean to brag, but we're already pretty well-known. Why not choose students who aren't?"

"Yeah," Ted agreed. "A lot of kids at Hillcrest aren't big in sports or honor students, yet they're right there yelling their hearts out at all the events."

Mr. Smiles beamed. "I felt I should ask, since it was your idea. Thanks for turning me down. Do you have any recommendations?"

Juli thought fast. "Someone from each class, maybe? Molly Bowen would be great for the juniors."

"Oh, yes. The quiet redhead with freckles like new pennies and enormous brown eyes," Mr. Smiles said. " 'Live wire' as a description is probably outdated, but I'll bet she's just that. I'll ask her."

"Can you beat that? He knows his students so well he can pick their faces out of thin air," Dave marveled when the minimeeting ended and Mr. Smiles had left. "Too bad every school in the country doesn't have a principal like him. Come on, Ted. You know how Coach gets when we're late for practice." He gave Juli's shoulders a quick hug and headed down the hall with Ted at his heels.

"We'd better get going, too," Shannon reminded. "I wish I'd driven today." She blew her black bangs from her forehead and ruefully admitted, "My Toyota's low on gas and I don't get my allowance until the weekend."

"Fancy being the daughter of a banker and still broke," Juli teased. "Won't Sean float you a loan?"

"Are you kidding?" Shannon opened her black-fringed eyes wider. "Dad gives me a good allowance, but when it comes to advances, he's a real Scrooge. I'd have been all right except I forgot my car needed servicing, then I saw this on sale." She stroked her sweater sleeve.

"So much for sales resistance. Get it? Sales, as in discount, marked down, forty percent off the last marked clearance price," Juli taunted.

Shannon speeded up. "Mercy me, enough already. I get it."

"Actually, it was worth it," Juli comforted. "The sweater makes your eyes look bluer." She followed her friend outside and to the city bus.

"Good to see you two," said Mr. Halvorsen, the friendly driver. He added his usual greeting: "Like I always say, one without t'other's—"

"—like ham without eggs," they told him, also as usual. Even though the joke had grown tiresome months earlier, they liked the kindly man and knew it pleased him for them to play along. They found a vacant seat and parked.

"I can hardly wait to call Ashley," Juli confided.

Shannon put on a droll expression. "That I should live to see the day!"

"There's a lot more to her than we thought," Juli defended.

"There usually is," Shannon agreed, with a knowing look.

That night Juli curled on a twin bed in her yellow room. The shiny dark eyes of her cinnamon-brown plush teddy bear, Clue, watched her from his home on her desk. Juli absently retied the red plaid ribbon around his neck. It had fastened the box he came in long ago. She patted her stuffed companion, took out the notebook she used to journal her most private thoughts, and grabbed a pencil. She wrote:

I am so thankful my junior year is going well. For the first time in ages, things have settled down. I don't have to be afraid. Or worried about Mom, Dad, or Shannon. Thanks for making things better, Lord, when no one else could. Now I can get back to writing my Christmas story. I want "More Than Tinsel" to show that Christmas isn't about things—it's that You loved us so much You sent Your Son Jesus to save us. If the story sells, someone may read it and learn about You. Maybe a girl like Ashley Peterson. She is just beginning to believe Christians don't have to be hypocrites.

The thought sent chills of responsibility up and down Juli's backbone. Her last waking thought was a prayer. *Please, Lord, help me do my best—for You.*

CHAPTER 3

When Juli Scott and Ashley Peterson became cocolumnists, they agreed to take turns writing their weekly young adult newspaper column. If both felt strongly about a certain subject, they would collaborate.

SVS—the Student Variety Show, as Molly Bowen and the other committee members from Hillcrest and Cove named it—fell into that category. The girls worked hard. They produced an article that frankly stated SVS was more than just a variety show. The sponsoring schools hoped to generate a new awareness of how diverse Bellingham residents really were. The finished column earned a grunt of approval from their editor, who only changed a few words.

The article sparked a flood of mail and phone calls. Many callers and writers praised the idea of developing closer relations between different ethnic groups and cultures. Others considered it unnecessary, even foolish. Some scoffed at the idea teenagers could promote community relations. Hadn't ministers and civic leagues been preaching the same thing for years? A few advised leaving well enough alone.

"Good grief," Ashley sputtered to Juli and their editor. "Sure we want to help build better relations, but it's also only a variety show! No one is forcing people to come. Why should they care if others do?" Her pale blue eyes flashed and she little resembled the girl with the flying brown hair who had resented Juli and Shannon a few months earlier.

The editor nodded and grinned. "I agree. I also feel an editorial coming on." The next edition of the paper carried a blistering editorial saying Bellingham and Whatcom County residents should be giving thanks for students who cared about their community. It ended with the words,

Caucasian or African-American, Asian or Native American. Scottish, Irish, German, or transplanted Canadian. Like it or not, we're here and we're here to stay. If you don't believe me, take a look at the people on the streets and in the malls. Check out your workplace and school. We represent the diverse heritage that characterizes America itself. Celebrate it, as our high school students are doing at their upcoming variety show.

"Isn't it wonderful?" Juli asked her lunch bunch. She glanced around the circle of friends that had begun with Shannon and herself. Dave Gilmore and Ted Hilton, grinning as usual. John Foster and Molly Bowen exchanging glances. A rather subdued Amy Hilton, far prettier now that she'd dumped the layers of makeup she used to wear. Carlos Ramirez, whose olive skin and curly dark hair highlighted his black velvet eyes and sparkling white smile.

"He sure tells it like it is. Some editors are afraid to rock the boat with editorials like this one," Dave said thoughtfully.

"What do you mean, rock the boat?" Juli challenged.

Carlos jumped into the discussion. "Obviously, not everyone's going to agree. People who don't agree cancel subscriptions and get the news from TV."

"So who needs them?" Juli said crossly, even though she knew he was right.

"Newspapers, dummy. How do you think papers pay for newsprint and ink and editors?" Ted teased. "No money, no news."

"Do you really think there will be percussions?" Shannon asked.

The lunch bunch burst into laughter. "You mean *re*percussions—widespread effects. Percussion makes a lot of noise, like drums."

"So? People who don't agree make a lot of noise, don't they?"

"Gotcha!" Ted chuckled. "Leave it to you to be least but not last."

Shannon stuck her nose in the air and haughtily told him, "Even I'm for knowin' it's 'last, not least,' Ted Hilton."

"I guess my Rileyisms just don't have what it takes," he admitted.

The bell signaling the end of lunch period rang and ended the sparring. Dave untangled his long legs from beneath the table. "We'll all be least *and* last if we don't watch it. Come on, Juli. I'll walk you to class."

She lengthened her stride and matched her steps to his. "Do you really think the editorial will make people cancel?"

Dave shrugged. "Who knows?" He grinned down at her, his eyes blue enough to swim in. "I wonder if you'll still want to be a writer after seeing what goes on behind the scenes at the newspaper."

"I hope to be a novelist, not a newspaper journalist," she corrected. She longed to tell him about "More Than Tinsel," but decided to hold off. Mrs. Sorenson, aka Allison Terrence, had talked with Juli about discussing her work.

"If you give away your plot before writing it, you lose the freshness you need for the first draft," she warned. "It's also far more heartbreaking to have a manuscript returned when everyone thinks it's wonderful and should be published. We're better off to keep mum until our work is actually printed."

Juli bit her lip. Waiting was hard, but her Honors writing teacher was right. She had turned the outcome of her Christmas story over to her Best Friend. Yet "thanks, but no thanks" would be far harder to accept if too many people knew about it. At present, only Shannon, the Scotts, and Mrs. Sorenson were aware of her current writing project. Telling Dave must wait.

At dinner, Juli continued the discussion from lunch. "Dad, do you think there may be 'percussions,' as Shannon called them?" She explained Shannon's latest mispronunciation.

To her surprise, neither Mom nor Dad laughed as heartily as she expected. Gary Scott's smile never reached his eyes. "There are a lot of people out there who won't like the editorial," he said. "I just hope it doesn't trigger anything worse than a few cancellations."

Juli's forkful of mashed potatoes stopped halfway to her mouth. Her stomach lurched at his tone of voice. "What do you mean?"

His face closed, showing he regretted speaking. "Maybe nothing."

Juli laid her fork across her plate. "I'm not a kid, Dad. I'm also involved with the newspaper. If something weird's going on, I have a right to know."

"It's just that there are a lot of militant groups out there," Mom put in. "You never know what they may do if someone angers them."

Juli felt like she'd just surfaced from a plunge into Bellingham Bay when ice clung to its shores. She knew about white supremacists, people who hated Jews and anyone else who wasn't fair-skinned like them. Who could help knowing? Every so often, TV newscasters reported some violent illegal activity. Hillcrest had a few boys with shaved heads who looked like they might belong to a neo-Nazi group. Other students avoided them. They swaggered through the halls and refused to participate in school activities, preferring to hang out with each other.

Dad sighed. "Western Washington has its share of fringe groups. Some are connected with those in Idaho. Every time a leader is arrested, another comes along. Or crawls out of the woodwork."

"Like the Children of Light, who kidnapped Shannon, only worse." Juli shuddered.

"Yes. They pledge themselves one hundred and ten percent to what they believe." His face darkened. "I wish every Christian were as dedicated to spreading the news of salvation as these people are to recruiting members! We'd have a revival so strong it would turn the earth upside down."

He forced a smile. "Enough gloom and doom. One good thing is coming out of all the evil in the world: Decent people who have sat back too long are being forced to take a stand. Some out of fear. Some from being shaken into realizing that if good people don't band together, things will continue to get worse. Law enforcement is only as good as the citizens it serves."

"You should write a letter to the editor," Juli said impulsively. "Not so much against groups, but letting readers know they need to wake up and do something. Your last sentence is a great theme: 'Law enforcement is only as good as the citizens it serves.' "

Dad stared at her and considered. "I may just do that, unless you and Ashley want to tackle the subject in your young adult column. Getting younger people involved is vitally important in making changes."

Juli felt the stirring of excitement that always came

with the beginning of something new and challenging. "Neat. I'll ask Ashley what she thinks."

"Why not give it a double whammy?" Mom suggested, blue eyes shining. "Juli's peers may not read letters to the editor. Adults may overlook the young adult column."

Ideas flew like seagulls before a storm. Quick phone calls won Ashley's eager approval and a green light from the editor. Before the Scotts went to bed, they had completed a rough outline for both Gary's letter and the girls' column. After Juli crawled into warm pajamas, she hugged Clue and wrote in her journal:

> *I am so glad Ashley and I are working for the newspaper, Lord. Even if I never sell a story or book, I feel we are making a difference with our writing, right here in Bellingham. A lot more people responded favorably to the column about the variety show than those who didn't care or hated the idea.*
>
> *I can hardly wait until tomorrow! Mr. Smiles said several kids have tentatively signed up to participate in SVS. Shannon promised an Irish folk song, and we're trying to talk Carlos into doing the Mexican Hat Dance. Molly asked the rest of the lunch bunch to help her with ticket sales.*

Juli tapped the end of her pencil against her notebook. She felt a smile turn up the corners of her mouth and went on writing.

*You're probably the only One who knows just
how great it is for me to concentrate on school
activities, instead of being in the middle of turmoil. I still like working on mysteries, but I must
admit, it's nice having time out! We all need it,
especially after everything that happened with
our Friday flight.*

She whispered a good-night prayer, turned out her light, and fell into an untroubled sleep.

Early the next morning, Juli received a disturbing call from the editor of the newspaper. "Thought you'd like to know my editorial brought in a load of mail and calls. Mostly positive; one anonymous." She felt a squiggle of fear go through her before he said, "The caller ranted against 'stupid fools cramming the insane idea of equality down the throats of those who are the only hope of saving America.' Probably a crank. He won't make me lay off, that's for sure."

Juli gulped. If she had received the letter, would she go on standing for right, the way she and Dad and Ashley were urging others to do? She just didn't know.

The newspaper editor couldn't have been more mistaken about the caller. That night, the city awakened to black night and a horrible BOOM, so violent it shook houses all over town. "Mom? Dad?" Juli struggled with her covers, automatically glancing at the digital clock. Large red numerals read 4:00. She freed herself and raced into the hall without bothering to turn on the light. Strong hands gripped her. She screamed in terror.

"Juli, it's Dad. You're all right." He reached for the light switch.

Relief turned her knees to spaghetti and she sagged against him. "What is it?"

"I don't know." Sharp creases etched themselves between his nose and lips.

"Gary? Juli?" Mom flew down the hall toward them. "What happened? It sounded like a bomb."

"I know," he said grimly. Long strides took him back down the hall to the master bedroom. In scant moments he reappeared wearing his uniform. "I'll be back as soon as I can. Turn on the TV and see if they have anything. Don't leave the house, no matter what." He disappeared out the kitchen door into the garage before Mom or Juli could move.

Juli swallowed hard. Dad never ordered his family around in that curt tone of voice unless he suspected danger. She dashed to the living room and grabbed the remote control. Mom followed. At first sight of the picture, Mom cried, "Dear God, no!" She turned so white, Juli forced her into a chair, dropped to the rug beside it, and glued her gaze on the TV set.

A flaming inferno filled the screen. The sound system faithfully reproduced the crackle and crash of burning timbers, the wail of fire engines.

"Wh-what is it?" Mom faltered. "The newspaper building?"

"Yes," Juli finally managed to gasp, her attention riveted on the horrendous scene. Cold sweat crawled over her body like a hundred snakes.

A reporter began her patter. "We're live at an out-of-control fire in the newspaper building," she announced. "The police have not disclosed details, but judging from the blast, it appears a bomb may have been planted."

Even in her misery, Juli noticed that the reporter used the words "appear" and "may have been." They provided an out if her speculations were proved wrong.

"Officers are urging people to stay away from the area and are ordering the crowd that has already gathered to go home. Several firefighting crews are working to keep the fire from spreading." The reporter stopped for breath. "There's no saving the newspaper building. Several surrounding structures remain in grave danger. Thank God there is little wind!"

The doorbell rang. A loud pounding on the front door followed. "Anne? Juli? It's Sean Riley and Shannon."

Juli hurried to let them in, surprised to see their van in the driveway. The noise of the TV had drowned the sound of the motor.

The tall, imposing banker with dark hair and blue-gray eyes so like his daughter's pushed into the hall. "Are you all right? We knew Gary wouldn't be here and thought you'd like company."

"We do." Anne held out a hand to each, but Shannon flew to Juli. Her eyes looked enormous. She started to speak. Juli's keen ears caught something on TV. She held up her hand to hush Shannon and ran back to the living room.

"We interrupt this live newscast with further breaking

news," a familiar anchorman declared. "Our station has just received a call from a man who claims to have planted the bomb that rocked Bellingham and destroyed the newspaper building." The reporter's voice hoarsened. Juli's nerves tensed.

"He warned more of the same will follow if, and I quote, 'stupid fools continue cramming the insane idea of equality down the throats of those who are the only hope of saving America.' "

"It's him!" Juli screamed. *"Those are the exact words the anonymous caller used after the editorial came out!"*

"Are you sure?" Sean demanded.

"Yes," Juli whispered through stiffened lips. "I couldn't forget them if I tried."

CHAPTER 4

The bombing of the newspaper office had startling results. Another paper offered temporary use of its facilities. "We refuse to be intimidated," the publisher of the flattened newspaper said. "If terrorists think they can silence the press, they'd better think again."

School administrators at Hillcrest and Cove met and hammered out an agreement also to stand firm, if the students agreed. "Canceling the variety show is giving in to pressure," an unsmiling Mr. Smiles told his student body. "I believe that every time it happens, it increases the chances of another incident. All in favor of holding the show, say aye." A deafening roar of approval rose.

"Nay?" Heads turned toward a small cluster of students with shaved heads who lounged just inside the auditorium door. Not a peep issued from them.

"Unbelievable," Juli told Dave. "I figured we'd get a bunch of nays."

He looked more serious than she'd ever seen him.

"They may have a reason."

"What kind of reason?" Shannon asked.

"I wish I knew." He shrugged. "Maybe they just don't want to call attention to themselves right now. Especially since the police announced that it's only a matter of time until they nab the creep who bombed the newspaper building then called in to the TV station and bragged about it." He wrinkled his forehead. "What a dumb move. You wouldn't expect it from a guy smart enough to build a bomb and plant it without being detected."

Juli's heart bounced to her throat. "You can't believe it's a Hillcrest student!"

"Not really, but I still don't trust those guys. According to rumors, they're involved in some pretty shady stuff."

"Hey, this is America," Shannon reminded. "People are supposed to be considered innocent until proven guilty."

"You got that right." Ted grinned at her. "Literally, to make a pun." When she groaned, he bowed and ushered her into the aisle and toward the door.

Dave waited until they were out of hearing, then told Juli, "It might not be a bad idea for Scott and Gilmore to do some unobtrusive P.I. work."

"Like what?" She asked, staring at him.

"Like keeping our baby blues turned in the direction of our head-shaved friends. Eavesdrop if we get the chance. Who knows?" He cocked an eyebrow. "We may hear something worth passing on to your dad or the Paynes. Andrew and Mary are sure to be involved in the investigation."

"I know." Juli thought of the red-haired FBI agent and his attractive wife. They had played a major part in her life ever since the mysterious Monday that turned her world upside down and set the stage for other mysteries. An uneasy feeling stole over her. The Paynes and Dad would be furious if she and Dave put themselves in danger by snooping, or hindered an investigation.

"Remember, no grandstand plays," Dave warned. "The radical element here at Hillcrest has kept low-key until now, but baby rattlesnakes do the same."

Suspicion flamed to certainty. "You really do think they're dangerous."

Dave shook his head. "I don't know if they're wanna-bes, Nazi sympathizers, or a bunch of guys trying to get attention. I do know no one in Bellingham is going to feel safe until the maniac who bombed the newspaper is doing time." He glanced at the auditorium, empty now except for themselves. "The best way we can help is to remember what you told me. God gave us two ears and one mouth. That means four ears between us. As the wolf-in-grandmother's-clothing told Little Red Riding Hood, 'the better to hear with, my dear.' "

He gave a believable imitation of a wolfish snarl, then laughed and gave her a quick hug. "To quote again, 'What big eyes you have, Grandmother.' Don't look so serious. Authorities aren't known for announcing pending arrests unless they're pretty sure they know the guilty parties."

"It could be to smoke out anyone else who's involved," Juli pointed out. "The idea of this being a one-person job sounds phony. It's too big. Too chancy."

"Unless someone's trying to make a name for himself, or is so full of hatred he can justify doing whatever he feels it takes to make people listen to him." Dave glanced at the wall clock. "We can talk later. Right now, the coach waits." He walked her to her locker where Shannon and Ted stood. "See you."

"See you," Juli echoed. She stuffed her backpack with the books she'd need to do homework and followed Shannon to the student parking lot and Shannon's red Toyota. Inside and seat-belted, she glanced at her friend. She hadn't even put the key in the ignition. "What are you waiting for?" Juli asked.

"Nothing." The dark-haired girl started the motor. "Actually, I'm still in shock over what Dave said. Do you think those boys are skinheads?"

"They could be," Juli said cautiously. She didn't want to break confidence by repeating what Dave said, so she added, "They could want attention and not know a better way to get it than by hanging out and looking tough." Her writer's imagination took flight. "Who knows what their homes are like? On the other hand, kids from great homes get involved in bad stuff, too."

Shannon put the car in gear and pulled into the street before she answered. "I know." Her voice thinned. "Sometimes I feel guilty for not inviting kids like that to come to our church youth group. They need to know God loves them."

Juli gulped. "Are you kidding? They'd flatten you!"

Shannon sighed. A brooding look came over her face.

"That's why I hesitate and never approach them. It's the old 'she who hesitates is last' thing."

"You mean, 'he or she who hesitates is lost,' " Juli mumbled.

Her friend shook her head. "They are the ones who will be lost. *I'm* last at having the courage to talk about God. Just call me the Cowardly Lion."

Juli squirmed. Shannon's frank admission that she wasn't brave enough to witness set sympathetic twinges fluttering and put Juli on the defensive. "I have a hard time just trying to be a good example," she muttered. "Besides, do-gooders who cram religion down kids' throats at school turn them off. Ashley Peterson used to think we were hypocrites."

Shannon grimaced. "We were."

"Honestly," Juli protested. "If we pranced up and began preaching to those boys, it would start a riot. They'd probably swear and call us obscene names."

Shannon stubbornly replied, "I'm not talking about prancing and preaching. I don't care about the names, either. People called Jesus names, but it didn't stop Him." She shook her head helplessly. "Why are we arguing, anyway? I won't be for approachin' anyone unless I find a lot more nerve than I have now."

She expertly guided the car around the corner that led to the Scott home, rolled down the street, and swung into the driveway. Mischief danced in her expressive eyes. "Want a thought for the day?"

"I have a feeling I'll get one, whether I want it or not," Juli grumbled.

Shannon grinned maddeningly. "Go to the head of the class."

"All right. What is it?" Juli climbed from the bucket seat of the Toyota and paused with one hand on the door.

All traces of laughter left Shannon's face. "It made a difference when Ashley got to know us," she said quietly. "Isn't that what the Student Variety Show is all about?" She didn't wait for an answer. The moment Juli stepped away, she eased the car into reverse and backed into the street.

That night, Juli thought a lot about what Shannon had said. She wrote in her journal:

> *It makes sense. Yet the idea scares me. None of the tough guys act interested in making friends outside the group and they're always together. No way will Shannon or I tackle the whole gang. Happy endings in that kind of situation only come on TV shows or in fantasy.*

A brilliant idea came into her mind like a flashbulb exploding.

> *What if I do as Dave suggested, Lord? If I listen to conversations, won't that also help me know whether the guys are for real? One thing, though. Right now, I'm like Shannon. I'll need a lot of nerve or some kind of sign from You before I'll even consider inviting a possible Nazi sympathizer to church. Or anywhere else!*

The city of Bellingham temporarily settled into uneasy peace. No further police comments about the bombing came forth. The first edition of the paper from its temporary home set tongues wagging. Under the words *Bellingham Banner* atop the front page, bold black headlines screamed "NAME CHANGE DEFIES ENEMIES." The article went on to say the new name had been chosen to reassure subscribers that the long-term policy of proclaiming truth would not be changed. Community leaders had been consulted and stood behind the decision 100 percent. The news story ended with the statement, "We refuse to be terrorized and we shall not allow a terrorist act to take away our right of free speech."

Inspired by the paper's actions, Juli and Ashley were all for going ahead with their citizens' responsibility article. Their editor issued a mighty "No!" He did promise to reconsider after the bomber was arrested and jailed. He also upgraded Gary Scott's letter to a half-page article, but ran it with a "Concerned Citizen" byline. Only the family, Ashley, and the Rileys knew who wrote it.

"Sometimes readers listen better if what they need to hear doesn't come from a police officer." The shrewd man gave Dad and Juli a wintry smile in a meeting on the Monday afternoon after the article came out. "You are a concerned citizen. Hopefully, so are our readers." He abruptly changed the subject. "How are ticket sales for your shindig, Juli? It's this Saturday night, isn't it?"

She grinned. Her short time with the crusty man had lessened her awe of him. "Yes." Her smile broadened. "Would you believe we're totally sold out?"

The editor grunted. "I'm not surprised. I don't recommend a bombing to stir up interest, but that's just what it did. We have a lot of outraged residents."

"Do we ever! Molly Bowen—she's in charge of tickets—says a large number of those who purchased seats said they never attend such affairs." Excitement went through Juli. "They're coming in protest against the bombing."

Tuesday passed. Wednesday, Thursday, Friday. Shannon had a haunted look on her face. "What if I forget the words to 'When Irish Eyes Are Smiling'?" she fretted in the Riley van on the way to the auditorium Saturday night. Her grandfather Ryan, aka Grand, had come into town from the Skagit House, and then the Rileys picked up the Scotts.

"Break into a jig," Grand advised with a chuckle. "Or just stand there and let the audience admire your Irish piper outfit. That pleated kilt of handwoven emerald wool is becomin'. So is the Irish Limerick lace on your white blouse."

"To say nothing of the green cloth square draped over your shoulder and pinned with a heavy Tara brooch," Mom put in. "It's gorgeous."

"You may win a prize for costume alone," Juli said. "If you do a jig, those enormous silver buckles on your black pumps will knock the judges' eyes out!"

"If I thought I'd be for winnin', I wouldn't sing," Shannon protested.

"We could all refuse to clap for you," Sean teased. It always surprised people when they learned how much humor lay hidden beneath what Shannon called his "banker look." He left his passengers at the door and went to find a parking spot. Three minutes after Sean dropped into his seat next to his shaky daughter, Mr. Smiles came to the microphone at one side of the platform and spoke to the multitude who had packed the room.

"Thank you for coming," he said simply. "You'll notice our participants are scattered throughout the auditorium. We wanted to make this as informal as possible, so that many nationalities can be represented." Juli gave a little bounce when he added, "Shannon Riley, our own Irish colleen who came to us a little over a year ago, will open our show."

She stumbled to her feet. "Pray for me," she pleaded in an agonized voice.

"We will, *mavourneen*—my little Irish darlin'," said Grand. "Knock 'em out!" he added, a twinkle in his eyes.

Applause burst out. Dave Gilmore leaned forward from the row behind Juli and said under cover of the clapping, "With that send-off, she'll be okay."

"You're in my way," his nine-year-old sister Christy complained.

"Lean back, son," Juli heard Dave's father say, then she turned her attention to Shannon. Her pale cheeks had grown red as wild strawberries, but she walked across the stage with an Irish lilt to her step. The accompanist played the introduction. Shannon opened her mouth, looked amazed when the first notes came out true and clear, then sang the plaintive melody. Juli saw

Grand blink hard when she finished. Shannon curtseyed, then ran back to her family.

The audience loved her.

They also loved an African-American group who gave a rousing performance, a Swiss yodeler, several Native-American dancers, and all the other students who had conquered fear to make a statement.

"Goody, I won't be for winnin' a prize," Shannon whispered to Juli halfway through the show. "The Japanese twins from Cove were adorable. What's next? Mercy me! Bagpipes and Scottish dancers doing the Highland Fling."

"The judges won't have an easy decision," Mom said when the dance ended.

"It's going to be a tough call, all right," Dad agreed.

Laughter bubbled from Juli like a waterspout at sea. "I don't think so. Look!"

Heads turned. A slim figure in traditional Mexican clothing came forward. The performer wore a serape over one shoulder and was topped by the most enormous braid-and-silver-trim hat Juli had ever seen. A wave of laughter and shouts followed his ambling progress. "Where's your donkey?" "Who are you, Pancho Villa?"

"Carlos Ramirez, is that you?" the Hillcrest principal asked.

"*Si,* Señor S–Miles." Students roared at the near slip of the new student's tongue, and Carlos sauntered onto the stage. The accompanist pressed the button of a tape recorder and started a song that set toes tapping and hands clapping. Carlos clicked his heels and began the

Mexican Hat Dance. His dark eyes and white teeth flashed. He bowed and leaped. He threw his bigger-than-king-size hat onto the stage and danced over and around it. The audience kept time. When he finished and sank to the stage with his big hat hiding most of him, the crowd went wild. Juli thought her eardrums would burst from the noise.

Dave poked her shoulder and pointed. Amy Hilton stood a few rows away. Happy tears poured onto her clapping hands. A sharp pang went through Juli. Carlos had been accepted tonight. Would it last? *Please God, let it,* she prayed.

"This concludes the competition part of our variety show," Mr. Smiles announced when the pandemonium died down. "We'll take a stand-and-stretch break before the judges' decision and our professional entertainment."

Before people could rise, a grating, unpleasant voice challenged, "The competition is far from ended. Be seated for the final act. Now."

CHAPTER 5

Heads turned. Mouths dropped open in disbelief. Shock rippled through the audience. Juli's hand flew to her mouth to hold back a cry of horror.

The tight-lipped boy who had spoken stood at military attention near the rear of the room. Juli recognized him, the boy who stood next to him, and two of the other six close behind, standing in military formation. All had shaved heads. All wore Nazi uniforms. Swastikas sprawled on caps and armbands like ugly black spiders.

Shannon's fingers dug into Juli's arm. Her face turned the color of ashes.

The very unexpectedness of the situation held the audience in screaming silence. Double ranked, the uniformed students came up the center aisle. They swung their arms and paraded in the goose step Juli recognized from World War II movie reruns. They passed Mr. Smiles, who stood frozen at the microphone. Then the stunned judges. The miniarmy paused, turned on their heels, and marched back down the aisle. Again heads turned. Horrified gazes followed the boys' progress.

Just before exiting, the leader snapped a salute. *"Heil, Hitler!"* he shouted.

"Heil, Hitler!" the other seven thundered in response. Then the steady tread of heavy boots faded and died in the hall.

At first no one moved or spoke. Gradually, a buzz began and grew to a din.

"This can't be happening," Juli protested.

Gary Scott's lips set in a grim line. "It just did."

"May I have your attention, please?" Mr. Smiles began, his voice hoarse. Conversation broke off and the audience turned toward him.

Juli glanced around her. Sympathy for the Hillcrest principal showed on many faces. *How would he handle the bizarre situation?* she had time to wonder before he spoke again.

Mr. Smiles' knuckles showed white against the microphone stand. "If you'll all be patient, the judges will confer then announce our winners."

"What a cool guy!" Dave muttered in Juli's ear. "Not one word about those jerks and their little performance. No wonder they didn't vote to cancel the show. They must have been planning this ever since Mr. Smiles announced it."

Juli nodded, rubbing the marks Shannon's clutching fingers had left on her arm. "How did they think they could get away with it?" she whispered to Dad.

He looked grimmer than ever. "Freedom of speech.

I'll explain later."

"Thank you for waiting," Mr. Smiles said when the judges had finished talking and handed him a slip of paper. He sounded more like himself. "I have an announcement before I read the winners' names. Because of the tremendous community support, it appears Cove and Hillcrest High will each receive several hundred dollars from tonight's proceeds. As far as I'm concerned, all who organized, participated in, and supported the Student Variety Show are winners."

He waited until the yelling subsided. "Now for the cash prizes. The third prize of $20 goes to the Swiss yodeler from Cove." There were loud cheers, especially among Cove students and parents.

"The Native-American dancers, also from Cove, take second prize—$35."

Juli noticed Ashley Peterson grinning at her from across the room and holding two thumbs up. Juli grinned back and clapped along with the rest.

Mr. Smiles glanced at the paper in his hand. "Our first place winner of $50 is. . ." A slow smile turned him back into the principal Hillcrest students respected and liked. Juli found herself clenching her hands into fists. If the judges had been insane enough to select the Nazi marchers, Mr. Smiles wouldn't look like that. *They were authentic,* her sense of fair play reminded. *Too authentic!* she mentally protested.

The principal's roving gaze moved on until it came to Juli, her family, and friends. Shannon cringed and slid down in her seat. She gave an audible sigh of relief when Mr. Smiles turned his attention to someone a few rows over.

"Will our Mexican Hat Dance performer, Carlos Ramirez, please—"

The crowd went wild. Whistling and screams of approval of the judges' decision drowned out the rest of Mr. Smiles's announcement. Eyes and teeth sparkling, Carlos went forward. When Mr. Smiles handed him the check, the migrant worker's son, who had captured the audience with his skillful grace, doffed the sombrero he had removed after performing and bowed to the judges.

"Would you like to say anything?" Mr. Smiles asked after the cheers stopped.

Carlos looked shy but took the mike. *"Si, señor. Gracias."* His smile flashed again and another storm of applause began.

It finally ended and the rest of the program began. Juli listened but wished it would end soon so she could talk with Dad. Did he suspect how she felt? Perhaps, for he whispered something to Mom. She nodded and fumbled in her purse. She took out pen and paper, wrote a note, and passed it and the pen to Juli.

The note read, "We'll go out afterwards. Friends are welcome."

Juli hastily scrawled "Yes!" and passed pen and paper back.

An hour later, the Scotts, Rileys, Gilmores, Thompsons, Hiltons, and assorted others swarmed into the Pizza Palace, one of their favorite haunts. Months had passed since the Wednesday a bank robber thought Juli and her friends had spotted him there. Tonight, though, only a few customers sat gobbling down what loyal patrons labeled the best pizza in Whatcom County.

The large group shoved tables together and ordered enough food to "feed the Marines," as Shannon put it, in between bites.

"Army, not Marines," Ted teased. The others laughed at her new Rileyism.

"Whatever." Shannon seldom allowed good-natured laughter to bother her. "Speaking of armies—"

"I thought we were speaking of Marines," Ted interrupted.

"You were the one who changed the subject, remember?" Shannon turned her back on her boyfriend and asked Dad, "I heard you whisper to Juli about freedom of speech. Is that why Mr. Smiles didn't say anything? And why you didn't arrest them?"

"I suspect your principal was too dazed to think clearly," Gary Scott said, his gray eyes dark. "He actually did the best thing possible under the circumstances, which was nothing. As for arresting them, they hadn't broken the law."

A wave of protest ran around the tables. "How can you say that?" Juli burst out. "Uh, sorry," she added when Dad raised an eyebrow. "It's just—"

"I know. Being reminded that kids today are still following Hitler's chilling teachings is frightening."

"Terrifying," Juli mumbled.

"It's not against the law for people to express their beliefs," Dad quietly said. "Especially in such a setting.

Democracy allows for people to make a statement without fear of arrest. The students did nothing to inspire hatred or start a riot. They simply took advantage of an invitation for different nationalities and ethnic groups to portray their heritage."

"How do we know they have German ancestors?" Dave Gilmore demanded.

Gary Scott looked around the circle of sober faces. "Such groups keep careful watch for loopholes. You'll notice only eight students marched. How many were from Hillcrest?"

Juli caught his unspoken message. "I recognized four of them."

"Out of how many shaved-headed boys who hang out together at school?"

Ted Hilton looked thoughtful. "A dozen, maybe."

"Exactly. I'll wager everyone in tonight's lineup has family ties to Germany. I'm sure whoever put them up to it—"

Shannon exclaimed, "You mean they weren't for thinkin' it up themselves?"

"Perhaps, but it's the kind of opportunity the leader of a group grabs with both hands. In either case, they could count on the element of shock. They'd also be smart enough to cover in case they were challenged. The best way to do that would be to include only those whose heritage qualified them to participate." He looked dead serious. "The wording also threw wide the door to what happened. Dressing up in Nazi uniforms and marching is not 'talent.' Doing so in recognition of their nationality loosely falls under the wide umbrella of 'variety.' I imagine future productions will be closely screened and require auditions."

"I'm glad Carlos won tonight," Amy Hilton said. "He deserved it." Juli noticed again how different she was. Amy used to consider every boy hers, and was only friendly toward girls when she wanted something.

"So are the rest of us!" Kareem Thompson chimed in. He and his wife Jasmine proudly looked at the young man who had come into their lives and home.

Carlos grinned and said, "If no one wants the last slice of pizza, I'll have it."

"Go ahead," they urged.

He reached for it. "Just call me Carlos the International. Can you beat it? A Mexican-American eating Hawaiian pizza in an Italian pizzeria!" The impromptu party broke up a short time later, with laughter and promises to see each other in church the next day.

Juli wrote in her journal before going to bed.

I know You love everyone, God, even people who do terrible things. I don't understand how they can be that way! I remember when I was in grade school and learned Hitler had ordered the killing of the Jews. It was hard to believe anyone could do that. I can't imagine being cooped up with so many people in a small space, like in "The Diary of Anne Frank." Or being afraid all the time the police would find our hiding place and take us away, too.

I hate even thinking about all the poor peo-
ple who died, but Dad and Mom say we need to
remember so it won't ever happen again.

Juli stopped writing. The same kind of thing was already happening in other countries. How lucky she was to live in America! The thought brought little comfort. Tonight, when those uniformed students marched in and took over the variety show, she had been sick with fear. She wrote:

It's not so much for my family and me—we're
white, so we are 'acceptable.' Hate groups are
against other races. African-Americans, like
Kareem and Jasmine Thompson. Jewish people
and those whose skin or religion is different
from theirs. I'm glad the students who marched
left before Mr. Smiles awarded the prizes.
Seeing Carlos win might have triggered them off
and led to real trouble.

Lord, sometimes I feel life is a Ferris wheel.
Just when I'm sky-high and on top of every-
thing, whoosh! Back down to the pits. Prejudice
and hatred are hurtful, even dangerous. It makes
me sad they will be around until Your Son
comes back. It isn't easy, God, but my family,
friends, and I are trying to make a difference.
Please help us. You're the only One who can.

She soberly put away her notebook journal. Yet the red

numerals on her digital clock marked off many minutes, more than an hour's worth, before she slept.

To the amazement of Hillcrest High students and staff, the four boys who participated in the variety show acted no differently than they had before. Juli exploded to Dave on the front steps of the school. "How come they aren't bragging? Or talking about the newspaper office bombing? I've been listening with both ears and all they talk about is the predictions for early snow this year. Hitler-lovers discussing the weather? Unbelievable!"

"That's suspicious in itself. Well, maybe not. Some of those groups are heavily into survival stuff and living in the woods." He glanced at the tightly closed ranks of the students with shaved heads who made up their own world within the world of Hillcrest High. "They give me the creeps. You never know exactly what they're thinking."

"Or plotting." Juli shivered and pulled her denim jacket closer, although the kindly autumn sun beamed warm rays from its perch on the western horizon.

Dave lowered his voice. "They also may have been warned to keep it down." Mystery drenched his words. "Carefully dropped hints by the police about far more than the self-confessed bomber being involved may be making them antsy." He caught at his slipping backpack and changed the subject. "Speaking of early snow predictions, I'm all for it. I can't wait to go skiing. I'm going to get my skis out and wax them this weekend. Need some help with yours?"

Dave's consideration was one of the things Juli liked

most about him. "Thanks, but would you believe Dad did ours two Saturdays ago?" She giggled. "I asked if he had reservations for us at the North Pole."

"What did he say?"

"He laughed and chalked it up to the 'be prepared' motto drummed into him when he was a Boy Scout."

Dave looked sheepish and mumbled something under his breath.

"You too?" Juli wanted to know.

"Sure. I'm an all-American boy and we all-American boys make sure we're prepared. Are you?"

"Am I what?"

He looked exasperated. "Prepared. For Honors writing class. Tomorrow is the deadline for our freelance stories. Nice of Mrs. Sorenson to let us choose our own subjects and styles. What are you writing, anyway?" His mouth stretched in a wide grin. " 'True Confessions of Juli Scott, Bellingham P.I.'?"

She shook her head. "No. A Christmas story I have to polish tonight. I finally got it written and checked between working on the variety show and everything else going on, but I'm not satisfied with it."

An hour later, she stared at a printout of "More Than Tinsel" and rated her work with the criteria Mrs. Sorenson had given her students. Plot: believable. Setting: accurate and specific. Characters: appealing. Theme: a natural part, not tacked on. Overall evaluation—Juli paused, unable to judge. She went back and reread the story, pretending to be Ashley Peterson reading it for the first time.

"Yes!" Juli said, grabbing her blue pen. Seeing "More

Than Tinsel" through her former enemy's eyes worked great. It showed up a weak spot and a clue to the resolution of the problem that needed to be made clearer. She scribbled her corrections, ran to the computer, made the changes, saved, and printed out a clean copy.

"Thanks, Lord. It's so good to finally finish my story. Will Mrs. Sorenson and the class like it?" A thrill of anticipation brought a smile to her lips. "If they do, I'll send it off to a youth church-school paper or magazine."

The following Monday, Juli mailed her story. The tips of her fingers felt damp. Did all wanna-be authors feel this way when mailing manuscripts? It wasn't her first try. Yet unless teacher, class, and her own heart were terribly wrong, "More Than Tinsel" was the best story she had ever written—and the most salable.

CHAPTER 6

"I feel like Alice in Wonderland," Juli confessed to Shannon on their way home from school the Thursday after she mailed her story. They had stopped for soft drinks. Now a rosy glow warned that darkness was nearly upon them. "Everything just keeps getting 'curiouser and curiouser.' "

"Yeah, *tell* me about it," her friend said before Juli could explain. Shannon's serious tone of voice erased Juli's other thoughts.

"What's happening and how come I don't know about it?"

"I wish I knew. Dad's been acting weird, too."

Juli tried to cheer her up. "It's hard to picture Sean Riley acting weird."

Shannon snorted. "Wouldn't you think it weird if your father cleared his throat and said you needed to talk, then clammed up? That's what Dad did last night. He had to leave for a meeting so I didn't get a chance to find out why. I was asleep by the time he got home."

Juli shifted position and faced Shannon. "I can't imagine your dad starting a conversation and not finishing it. Do I smell a mystery?"

The Irish girl looked worried. "Maybe. He sure acted strange." She turned a corner and went on, "I know he's really busy at work. They had to fire an employee recently. Dismissals always bother Dad. He takes it personally if anyone in his bank has to be let go."

Juli considered for a moment. "You already know about that, so it can't be what Sean started to tell you. What else has he done that's weird?"

"He bought three new suits."

Juli laughed. "Your dad is a banker. Wearing suits to work is tough on them. Besides, if buying new clothes makes a person weird, we're in trouble!"

Shannon's lips set in a straight line. "Excuse me for thinking my best friend would understand," she said sarcastically.

Juli's laugh died. Sarcasm and Shannon normally didn't belong on the same planet. "Sorry. I didn't realize how upset you were. I just don't see—"

"Eat dinner with us tonight and you will."

"Sure, if we can stop at home and tell Mom. I also want to check the mail."

Juli's innocent request chased away Shannon's gloom. Her eyes twinkled and she dropped into the brogue she used to tease her friends. "Mercy me! You submit a story on Monday and are for expectin' an answer before the glue on the envelope dries. 'More Than Tinsel' is good, but a three-day turnaround? Get real."

Juli felt hot color pour up from the collar of her jacket. "Excuse me for thinking my best friend would understand," she mimicked. Their shared laughter cleared the air. Juli added, "It can happen. Remember Mrs. Sorenson telling about the author who sent the first and only chapter of a novel she had written to a New York publisher? She received a letter by return mail."

"Asking to see the rest of the novel!" Shannon finished the story. "Mrs. Sorenson said the author uses it when she teaches and speaks. She calls it her horrible example." She pulled into the Scotts' driveway. Colored leaves that had fallen since the last raking dotted the emerald lawn. "Want me to come in?"

"If you want to." Juli secretly hoped she wouldn't. The chances of hearing from the magazine this afternoon were not much above zero, but when she did, she wanted to be alone. Rejections for other stories had been bad enough, but because she had poured so much more of herself into the Christmas story, getting it back couldn't help being hard. She stubbornly raised her chin. If or when it came, she'd send it out again. Look how long it had taken Dad to sell his story, "Murder in Black and White."

"Come back, come back, wherever you are," Shannon chanted. "I said I'd wait in the car." She stretched as much as the bucket seat allowed. "Take your time. It's neat out here. I love autumn."

"So do I." Juli glanced at leaves swirling down. "It's the *fall* of the year."

Shannon groaned. "Your puns are worse than my Rileyisms," she complained. "Hurry up, will you? I have a roast to get started or there won't be any dinner."

Juli climbed from the red Toyota and ran lightly to the door. "Mom?"

"Right here." Anne Scott appeared, wearing a favorite sweat outfit.

Juli hugged her. "It's nice not to have to use my key. Okay if I eat at Shannon's? It's short notice, but she really wants me to come." She held back the words on the tip of her tongue. Telling Mom Shannon thought her father was acting weird would start a long discussion, as well as betray her friend's trust.

Mom arched her eyebrows and teased, "You must have known we're having leftovers. I stayed at school this afternoon to do some work in the library and only got home a few minutes ago." She headed back to the kitchen.

Juli slowly walked toward the table where they put the mail. The corner of a large tan envelope sent her heart to her throat. She snatched it from the pile and relaxed when she saw it was addressed to her parents.

A quick survey of the rest of the mail showed no envelope that might contain an acceptance and check, so Juli trailed Mom to the kitchen. "If I'd known you were going to be late, I'd have come straight home and started something."

"No need. Dad likes spaghetti pie better the second day."

"Don't let Shannon hear the words 'spaghetti pie' or we'll never get away," Juli warned. "She likes it even better than pizza." She started back to the front door but hesitated long enough to say, "Has Dad said anything more about the variety show or the newspaper building bombing?"

Mom shook her head. "No, and I haven't asked." Her direct gaze met Juli's. "We both know he will tell us what he can when he can." She took salad makings from the fridge. "I suspect the authorities are lying low in hopes the guilty person or persons will get nervous and give themselves away."

"I hope so. See you later."

"Right. Have a good time." Mom wrinkled her nose. "As if you wouldn't!"

Juli repeated Mom's comment to Shannon on the short drive to the Riley home. To her surprise, Shannon barely smiled. When they reached the kitchen and started making dinner, she said, "Do me a favor and really watch Dad. Okay? Maybe I'm the weird one around here."

"Maybe," Juli agreed, after Shannon's lips twitched. "I will watch, though."

"You'll tell me honestly what you think?"

"When haven't I been honest?" Juli demanded.

"Never," Shannon admitted. "I just don't want you to start now. Especially now," she added, half under her breath. "It could be really important."

A tiny alarm rang in Juli's brain. With it came the feeling something unusual lay ahead. She thought of the times such a feeling proved to be right. She also admitted it had meant nothing an equal number of times. Which would it be this time? A false alarm or a warning bell?

Juli fixed her gaze on Sean and concentrated all during dinner. She didn't realize just how intently until Sean said, "Do I have something on me? You're staring as if you'd never seen me before, Juli."

She blushed and stammered about admiring his new suit, thankful Sean had arrived home late and not bothered to change before dinner.

Sean laughed. His blue-gray eyes so like his daughter's sparkled with mischief. "Thanks. I had several compliments today."

From women? Any widower so tall and attractive received a lot of attention from the opposite sex. Sean's being a banker added to his eligibility, a fact recently demonstrated by the pursuit of a scheming, unscrupulous woman who had turned a Scott-Riley family vacation into a nightmare.

Juli smiled to herself. Shannon's father was far too shrewd to be taken in. He would also never remarry unless he felt God had sent a real Christian woman into his life, someone who would love Shannon as well as himself.

In spite of her super sleuthing, Juli saw nothing strange about Sean. She told Shannon so while clearing the table and loading the dishwasher. "Looks like you worried for nothing."

"I hope so. He acted totally unweird tonight."

"What kind of word is that? Who ever heard of 'unweird.' "

"Well, 'uncool' wasn't a word, either, until someone said it first and made it popular." Shannon grinned. "New words get put in the dictionary all the time."

"What you said earlier was right," Juli told her. "If there's anyone weird around here, it's you!"

"Yeah. I'll drive you home. Be right back, Dad," she called from the door into the living room. Juli stood just behind her.

"Good." Sean cleared his throat. "We need to talk. Good night, Juli."

"Good night." She followed Shannon out.

"So much for unweird. That's the second time he's done that," Shannon said, sliding behind the wheel. "He's driving me crazy! Don't try to cheer me up. Something is bugging Dad. Period."

Juli got in the car. "Tell him when you get home. You're going to explode if you don't." She didn't add that something in Sean's voice had set the alarm bell clanging in her own mind, too. The last thing Shannon needed was to deal with a sometimes-right, sometimes-wrong warning system in Juli's brain!

At 10:30, Shannon called. Juli was in bed but not asleep. Shannon said, "I'm driving tomorrow and will pick you up." Her guarded tone of voice told nothing. Sean must be near the phone. Shannon lowered her voice. "Everything's cool, I think." She hung up, leaving Juli staring at her phone.

"Well, how do you like that?" she asked Clue. His bright black gaze gave no more information than Shannon's cryptic message had. She laughed. "You're a good companion, Clue. My secrets are safe with you.

"They are a whole lot safer with God," she quickly added. "You're nice, but only a stuffed bear. God is real.

I just wish more people knew that." She yawned. "No journal writing tonight." She turned out her light, said her prayers, and tried to figure out what was going on with the Rileys.

Early the next morning, Shannon pulled up in her car. Juli crawled into the passenger seat and buckled herself in, glad for the warmth of the heater. Each fall morning grew a little colder. Juli picked up the conversation right where Shannon had left off the night before. "What did you mean when you said everything was cool, then added, 'I think'?"

"Just what I said." Shannon's cheeks showed scarlet above a red turtleneck. "Dad hasn't come down with some horrible disease. He hasn't stolen funds from the bank. He hasn't—"

"Stop with the hasn'ts," Juli ordered. "Just tell me what's going on."

"Never interfere with a driver," Shannon droned in the monotone their driver's education instructor used when they took the course. She relented and switched to her normal voice. "You know the Thanksgiving dinner our church is sponsoring for those who don't have family or friends close by?"

"Sure. Our families decided to give up our own Thanksgiving and help. How does that make your dad weird?" Juli impatiently asked.

"He invited the new bank employee to our church and to the Thanksgiving dinner. She transferred from an Everett bank because it meant a promotion."

"Is that all? No big deal." Juli relaxed. So much for her premonition.

"It may be a bigger deal than we think," Shannon said. "I haven't seen Dad this happy since Mom died." She fell silent. "I'm glad, but something bothers me. Dad said he asked Emily Carr several days ago. Why didn't he tell me?"

"Probably because he didn't know how you'd react. How *did* you?"

"You mean did I rage like a jealous stepdaughter-to-be?" Shannon laughed for the first time since they left the Scott place. "The answer is no. I asked what the new employee was like. Did I ever find out! Seems like she's loyal, efficient, courteous, and all those other things kids in scouting promise! I didn't have the nerve to ask if she's beautiful. We can find out Sunday. She and her daughter are coming to church." Shannon sighed. "It should be interesting."

Juli echoed the remark to her parents that night. Shannon had shrugged and said everyone else would know about it soon, so the Scotts might as well be informed ahead of time. "I hope she's as nice as her name," Juli said. "Emily Carr is kind of a friendly name. She has a fourteen-year-old daughter named Jessica, who is in a wheelchair. Jessica hasn't walked since the car crash that killed her father a couple of years ago."

"It seems to me the Carrs can use all the love and friendship our church can offer," Anne Scott said in her quiet way. "I'm glad we know a little of the background. It always helps to understand." Juli nodded in agreement.

She felt even more glad when the Carrs showed up at church Sunday. Juli fell in love with Emily at first sight. She was close to Juli's and Shannon's height, with short, light-brown hair. Tiny lines that Juli recognized came from pain and loss, added to, rather than detracted from, her attractiveness. So did the peace that must have been hard-won, and her simple, "I am glad to meet you all" when Sean introduced her.

Jessica was a short, charming younger edition of her mother. The shadow in her brown eyes even when she smiled went straight to Juli's heart. Shannon blinked hard and Juli realized her friend felt the same. In spite of Jessica's smile, her eyes held a reaching-out, a please-accept-me expression that won instant sympathy.

The senior high youth group responded to that unspoken plea with genuine welcome. So did the Thompsons. The haunted look in Jessica's gaze lessened. It returned when Kareem announced, "I have great news. Friends have offered the use of a cabin near Mount Rainier for a youth retreat the first snowy weekend we have. The cabin is quite isolated, and up a winding mountain road. You'll join us, won't you, Jessica?"

Juli clenched her hands. Anger spurted. She couldn't believe Kareem had been so insensitive. How could a girl in a wheelchair go on a winter retreat?

Jessica ducked her head. "I–I don't know if I can," she whispered, her voice loud in the suddenly silent room.

"Of course you can," Dave Gilmore and Ted Hilton said at the same time. Ted flexed his muscles, grinned, and said, "Think two macho men like us can't handle one girl and a wheelchair?"

"Are you sure?" Jessica's uncertain expression added, *Are you sure I won't be a nuisance and in the way?* It made Juli wonder how she had been treated by those who knew her before she came to Bellingham.

"Ted's just waiting for a chance to show off how strong he is. So am I," Dave confessed. "Don't even think of not giving us the chance by staying home."

The look of disbelief and gratitude on Jessica's face made Juli's heart ache.

CHAPTER 7

The following Thursday night, Juli punched in Ashley Peterson's telephone number with impatient fingers. The phone rang once, twice, three times. Of all the times for Ashley not to be home! Just when Juli had fantastic, marvelous, stupendous news. "Almost as good as selling my story," she muttered.

A breathless voice interrupted the fifth ring. "Hello?"

"It's Juli. You sound like you've been running."

"Hold on, will you?"

"Sure." Juli beat time on the arm of her chair while waiting.

A few minutes later Ashley came back on the line. "Sorry. I just got out of the shower. My hair was dripping down the back of my neck. What's happening?"

Juli could picture the other girl, her head wrapped in a towel. "Just the greatest ever. What are you doing this weekend?"

"Why?" Caution edged the blunt question.

Juli grinned. Since working with the junior from Cove, she'd learned Ashley Peterson never committed herself until she knew all the details. "There's a really early snow on Mount Rainier," she explained. Anticipation spilled over into her words. "Our church youth group is having a mountain retreat. We're leaving tomorrow after school. I just found out about it. Can you go?"

After a short silence, Ashley said, "I don't belong to your youth group."

"So what? Neither do some of the other kids. We're allowed to ask friends. The best thing about it is that the retreat is free. We had a fund-raiser last summer. There's enough in our treasury to pay for food and gas."

"What is this, a Bible-thumping, convert-the-visitors weekend?" Ashley asked.

Juli's laugh bubbled over. "No. We'll sing and have devotions, with some kind of a lesson Sunday morning. Those who want to will have time to share, but no one will beat you over the head with a Bible. I promise."

Ashley's suspicion evidently faded, for she giggled. "That's a relief!" Her voice changed again. "Who's going? If it's a couples thing, count me out. Ditto if it's all skiing. I'm not into that, but I like sledding."

"It's never just couples with the Thompsons as chaperones. It's like one big happy family, with plenty of fun activities for everyone. Dave Gilmore's folks have plans, so he's bringing his little sister, Christy. Jessica Carr, whose Mom just started working at Sean Riley's bank, is also coming. You'll love her. She's in a wheelchair and—"

"Wheelchair!" Juli could almost hear the wheels turning in Ashley's brain.

"Yeah. Dave and Ted Hilton promised to give her whatever help she needs. The rest of us will, too. There will be as many kids sledding and building snowmen as skiing. Can you come?" Juli paused. "We really would love to have you."

" 'We' meaning who?" Ashley asked.

"Shannon and I." Juli fought back irritation. Why did Ashley have to be so suspicious? "The other kids will, too, once they know you're coming." She tried the light touch. "Check your calendar and see how many social engagements you can wipe out, will you? This is going to be megafun."

"I'll have to call you back after I talk to Mom." A certain reserve crept into Ashley's voice. She hesitated. "Is everyone showing up in designer ski clothes?"

"Amy Hilton probably will," Juli said frankly. She laughed when Ashley mumbled, "Why doesn't that surprise me?" then went on. "The rest of the kids will wear anything they have that's warm. My ski suit was a Christmas present from Shannon's father and grandfather last year." She laughed again. "Yellow and black. I look like a bumblebee on the slopes."

To her delight, Ashley cut in with, "If you'll hang up, I'll check with Mom and call you back."

"Well! I can take a hint, as the Irishman said after being kicked downstairs for the third time," Juli told her.

Ashley groaned. "That remark shows you've been hanging out with Shannon too long." She broke the connection, but called back less than five minutes later.

"Mom said yes. Where do we meet and when? What should I bring?"

"Meet us at the church right after school." Juli gave the address. "Bring warm clothes, sleeping bag or thick blankets. There are only a few beds, so most of us will sleep wall-to-wall on the floor. We also need our own soap and towels. Everything you need to camp out, although Shannon insists it should be called a camp *in,* since we won't actually be outdoors."

"Sounds like her." Ashley chuckled. "Uh, thanks for inviting me, Juli." She gave a short laugh but sounded choked up.

Juli could sense the other girl wanted to say more. Something like, *I can't believe this is happening. I never dreamed Juli Scott would invite me to anything, let alone an all-expenses-paid mountain weekend.* Someday Ashley might be able to say it. For now, her accepting the invitation was enough.

Juli hung up the phone and called Shannon and Kareem Thompson to let them know Ashley could go, then ran to pack her gear. There wouldn't be time tomorrow after school. She also took time to write in her journal.

Please help us make Ashley feel welcome, Lord.
Something has turned her off to Christians.
This is a chance for her to see that even though
we make lots of mistakes, You forgive us and
encourage us to try to do better.

The next afternoon, a swarm of buzzing students filled the church parking lot. Juli's heart pounded with excitement while Kareem and the boys loaded a mountain of belongings into the church bus. "Aren't you glad you came?" she exclaimed to Ashley, trim in jeans and a winter-patterned slipover sweater.

Ashley rolled her eyes. "Of course. Church parking lots are one of my favorite places to hang out." Her wide grin took the sting from her sarcastic remark. "Do they really expect to get all that gear and all of us in one bus?"

"I was wondering the same thing," a doubtful voice echoed from behind them. Juli turned. "Jessica! I'm so glad you're here." She smiled at Emily Carr, standing beside her daughter's wheelchair. If the older woman had qualms about the weekend, she wisely kept them to herself. Juli suspected she was the kind of mother who would bite her tongue rather than suggest that Jessica couldn't do things.

"This is my friend and cocolumnist, Ashley Peterson," Juli said. "Mrs. Carr and Jessica."

The girl in the wheelchair lit up like a Fourth of July firecracker. "All right! I love your column in the *Banner*. It is so cool. I never knew real authors before."

Her honest praise cut through Ashley's protective armor like a Swiss Army knife through soft cheese. The invited guest knelt until her eyes were on a level with Jessica's admiring face. "Thanks. Since Juli and I got to know each other better, I guess we make a pretty good team."

"Pretty good? You guess?" Jessica scoffed. "You're

the best, especially on the columns you do together." She stopped and looked wistful. "Do you think you could write a column about people like me sometime? Not me, exactly, but what it's like to be in a wheelchair—the way other people treat you." She leaned forward in her eagerness to explain.

"I got the idea from an article in *Focus on the Family* called 'Seven Things Disabled Kids Want You to Know.' The author, Anita Corrine Donihue, used headings that fit teens as well as little kids. She talked about the importance of accepting people for who they are and letting them do their best, not just feeling sorry for them." Jessica looked exasperated. "I get so tired of people seeing my wheelchair and not me! I'm the same person I was before the car wreck!" She giggled. "Only older, of course."

A look of awe crept over Ashley's face at Jessica's frank confession. Determination followed. "If our editor says okay, how would you like to co-coauthor an article with us?"

Jessica's brown eyes shone. "I'd leap at the chance." Another giggle came. "Change that to *roll* at it." She tore her gaze free from Ashley's face. "What do you think, Juli?"

Juli bent down and pretended to retie a shoelace. She needed time to hide the quick tears Jessica's valiant spirit brought. She also needed time to evaluate what she sensed happening between Ashley and Jessica. With a quick prayer for guidance she slowly straightened. "Great idea, but I have a suggestion."

Ashley's lip curled and she started to speak. The look in her eyes shouted disappointment that her cocolumnist hadn't simply praised the idea and kept her suggestions to herself.

I don't blame her, Juli soberly thought. *If I were in her shoes, I'd feel the same way.* She hurriedly said, "I really do like your idea, Jessica, but I'm snowed under with other things right now. Why don't you and Ashley go ahead and do the article, instead of waiting for me?"

Jessica looked anxious. "I don't want to butt in. It's your column." She glanced appealingly from Juli to Ashley, who acted as if she'd gone into shock.

"Hey, having you and Ashley work together is my idea, remember?" The expression in Ashley's face rewarded Juli far beyond losing the chance to help write a meaningful story.

"All abooaard," Ted Hilton trumpeted through his loosely clasped hands. He and Dave loped toward the Carrs, Juli, and Ashley. A smiling Shannon followed at a more leisurely pace. "Ready, Jessica?" Ted grinned at her.

"Yes!" Her hands shot up. "See you, Mom."

Emily Carr hugged her daughter, then watched her roll forward, flanked by the tall basketball players. "Thank you so much," she told the three girls. Her brown eyes so like her daughter's focused on Shannon. "You'll look after her?"

"I will. She'll be sound and safe." When Emily looked startled, Shannon sighed. "Mercy me! Did I get it backwards? I'm sorry."

"At least the sorry part is right," Juli teased. "Mrs.

Carr, Shannon has misquoted and mispronounced most of the words in the English language. We call them Rileyisms."

"I'm not that bad," her friend protested. "We really will bring Jessica home sound and safe."

Mrs. Carr looked deep into the honest gray-blue eyes. "I'm sure you will." Her confidence turned Shannon's cheeks a lovely pink. She patted the Irish girl's arm and sent a grateful glance toward Juli and Ashley. "If you feel comfortable with it, I'd like you to call me Emily."

"I wish you and Sean and Mom and Dad were going with us," Juli impulsively said. "They usually help chaperone, but this came up so suddenly, they weren't available. Not that Kareem and Jasmine can't do the job," she added.

"Of course they can. I'm also tied up this weekend, but maybe I can go another time." Emily's smile was like seeing a light turned on. "Have a good time." She walked toward the bus and stood beneath the window next to the seat where the boys had deposited an ecstatic Jessica.

"She's nice," Ashley commented. "They both are." She turned accusingly to Juli. "How come you're too busy to work on Jessica's article?"

Juli felt thrilled at Ashley's referring to the unwritten article as Jessica's. She looked straight into the other girl's skeptical eyes. "I have the feeling you need to work together without me. I'd love to help write the article," she confessed, "but when you knelt down and talked with Jessica, it was like something special happened between you. Do I sound dumb?"

Ashley's mouth dropped. Her face turned scarlet. After a long moment she said, "No. You don't sound dumb." She turned and ran toward the bus.

"That's it?" Juli felt bitterly disappointed.

Shannon hugged her. "It's a whole lot, coming from Ashley." She sounded sympathetic. "Just agreeing to come on our winter camp in is a 180 degree turnaround for her. Don't expect Ashley to say what she's feeling. Give her time, Juli. She needs to get used to us. I'd guess not many people step aside and give her a chance at something she desperately wants."

"Which number sermon is this?" Juli taunted, knowing Shannon was right.

Her friend refused to be baited. "You weren't the only one to recognize the special moment between Ashley and Jessica. The feeling of instant friendship may never have happened to her before." Her eyes clouded with memories. "We're lucky. We both felt it the day Mr. Smiles asked you to show a terrified Irish immigrant around Hillcrest."

"When I barely knew my way to the girls' room," Juli put in. "I'll never forget your saying it was like the blind leading a friend."

"My very first Rileyism," Shannon reminded, with a ripple of laughter. "And your very first time correcting me!"

"Are you two coming?" Ted bellowed.

The girls smiled in perfect understanding. "Yes!" they yelled, and raced toward the crowded bus. Christy Gilmore and Jasmine Thompson sat just behind Kareem, who was driving. Juli and Shannon sat together with Dave and Ted just behind where they could lean forward and talk with the girls. Juli had told her friends about Ashley's comment concerning couples. The boys agreed to play it cool. "We can be together other times," Dave said.

"Like on the slopes." Ted gave a Cheshire cat grin. "Ashley doesn't ski."

"I don't think it will matter." Shannon nodded at two brown heads showing above a seat a few rows ahead. "Ashley zoomed in on Jessica like a missile locked onto a target."

Juli leaned forward, trying to catch a few words above the steady hum of conversation in the bus. She sat back, satisfied. "Just what I suspected. They're already discussing their article for the *Banner.*" Great! Why had she blurted that out? What if the editor hated the idea?

"Article? What's up, Juli? Are you being replaced already?" Dave teased.

"No." She quietly explained and made them promise secrecy. "If a bunch of people know about it and it doesn't happen, the girls will feel even worse."

"I know what you mean," Ted solemnly agreed. "I tried out for a snowman part in a play in second grade, but only got to be a chipmunk. It nearly crushed me."

"Chipmunk suits you better," Shannon told him unsympathetically. "You really are a nut."

Dave and Juli howled. He patted her shoulder and she smiled at him. What a great day! Good friends. A retreat. Ashley and Jessica part of it. How much better could life get? Even the gray skies and light rain over Interstate 5 meant more snow in the mountains. Juli reached for Dave's hand and squeezed it, wondering if anything could ever be more perfect than the present moment.

CHAPTER 8

Darkness hung just above the horizon when the church youth group and their friends reached the log house near Mount Rainier. "Pinch me so I'll know it's real," Juli told Shannon. She stared at the snow-topped building set against a backdrop of dark green trees frosted in thick white. Surrounding ridges and slopes looked purple in the growing dusk.

"It looks like a Christmas card," Shannon agreed. "Good thing we haven't gone back on standard time yet, or it would be blacker than sin right now."

"Shannon Riley, you are something else!"

A gray-blue gaze turned toward her. "What did I say wrong this time?" the Irish girl meekly asked, although mischief danced across her face.

"Nothing," Juli reluctantly admitted. "It's just that a person doesn't think of sin in such a clean and beautiful place."

"Okay," she said, adding in a loud whisper, "Shhh.

Kareem's making an announcement."

Their handsome leader slid a dark jacket over his blue sweatshirt. "I know you want to make the most of the daylight that's left," he told his excited passengers.

"How did you guess?" Ted Hilton asked in a solemn tone. Everyone howled.

Kareem sent a laughing glance at his wife. "Jasmine and I do, too. We need to get our gear inside, but we can sort it out later." Groans turned to cheers, and the youth leader added, "Jessica, will you stay in the bus and supervise? This crew needs all the help it can get!"

Ashley Peterson blinked, but Juli gave her a private two-thumbs-up signal. Understanding sprang to Ashley's face. Putting it that way instead of making a big deal about Jessica staying in the bus until Kareem got the cabin warmed up was a smart move.

It paid off. The uncertainty that lurked in Jessica's brown eyes faded. "Sure. Then Dave and Ted can haul me inside."

"No way!" Dave retorted. "Don't think that wheelchair is going to keep you out of a snowball fight. We'll throw a cushion on a waterproof tarp and you can roll snowballs for ammunition, if you don't want to throw for my team."

"Who says you get to be captain? And if you are, who says you get to choose first?" Ted loudly complained. "If Jessica's sitting on the ground, she can reach the snow a lot better than the rest of us who are tall!"

The whole busload of students burst into laughter when Christy Gilmore tugged at Ted's sleeve and cried,

"So can I! I'm short." She danced up and down. "I'll be on your team, Ted."

"Thanks a lot, Christy," her brother grunted. "I planned to choose you."

"When? After Jessica and Juli and Ashley and—"

Dave made a dive for her, but she nimbly stepped behind Jasmine.

Jessica laughed until tears sparkled on her lashes. She pretended to crack a whip. "Move it, slaves. You heard what Mr. Thompson said."

Kareem smiled at her. "When people call me 'Mr. Thompson,' it makes me think of my foster father. We're strictly first names around here, Jessica."

Surprise showed in Ashley's face again. She obviously hadn't expected such friendly informality between the youth and their leaders. "I'll make sure to take your stuff," Ashley told Jessica. "Guys bang everything around —especially guys in a hurry," she said as Dave and Ted collided in the aisle.

"You get the service you pay for," John Foster called from behind them. Molly Bowen's laughing, freckled face peered around his arm.

"Right," Shannon put in. "Nothing plus nothing equals zero."

Juli didn't bother to tell her it was "equals nothing." Her friend would only look innocent and point out that zero *was* nothing. Strange. Shannon's Rileyisms always made sense, sometimes even more sense than the sayings she misquoted!

Minutes later, warmly dressed figures spilled from the

golden glow of the bright cabin interior. "No skiing or wandering off tonight," Kareem reminded. "Also, no sledding until we check out the slopes. We'll pick one in the morning; maybe even lay a bonfire for tomorrow night." He grinned at the eager faces. "Since Dave and Ted already have begun the selection process for Operation Snowball, we'll let them be captains. Choose up, men."

Juli suspected they had made their choices ahead of time. Ashley and Shannon wound up on Dave's team along with Jessica and several others. Juli joined Christy on Ted's team. The Thompsons volunteered to prepare the night's meal. "Only if we don't have to do anything else this weekend," Jasmine warned. "Everyone plays. Everyone eats. Everyone cleans up."

"Is that the way you always do it?" Ashley whispered to Juli on her way to join the others. Her face glowed above her heavy turtleneck and thick jacket.

"Uh-huh. It isn't fair for the chaperones to get stuck with the work. Something else isn't fair, either." She yelled to Dave, "That silver and black ski suit blends into the shadows. How can I see you?"

"Is it my fault your jacket's bright yellow?" he teased. "Cheer up. Tomorrow when the sun shines, you'll look like a leftover autumn leaf."

Juli bent, scooped snow into a soft, loosely packed ball, and hurled it in his direction. Splat! A shower of flakes spattered his face. "The enemy has fired the first shot," Dave bellowed. "War is declared. Start making ammunition, Jessica!"

They played in the snow until night surrounded them and the spicy smell of pasta lured their grumbling stomachs away from the snow fight. Bright-eyed and rosy-cheeked, they stormed to the porch. Kareem met them at the door.

"Kick off your boots and brush off your snowy clothes here," he ordered. "Boys change upstairs in the bedroom. Girls use the one down here." His dark eyes twinkled. "Don't get any ideas about who will sleep in the beds. Jasmine and I already decided that. I get the bed upstairs. My charming, spaghetti-making wife gets one of the twin beds down here."

"Why are we not surprised?" Amy Hilton said. Juli searched for signs of discontent over having to sleep on the floor but found none. Amy's comment was simply what any of the others might have made to Kareem.

Their leader grinned at her. "The second downstairs bed goes to our hardworking ammunition maker." He bowed ceremoniously in Jessica's direction. "She did all the work while the rest of you threw her snowballs."

"And fine snowballs they were for bein'," Shannon added.

"Hey, you with the Irish brogue. You're dripping," Ted said.

"So are you. Someone get a mop, please."

Supper proved filling and hilarious. Quantities of spaghetti, warm garlic bread, and tossed salad vanished like snow in July. So did the bag of homemade cookies sent by Anne Scott. Juli missed Mom, Dad, and Sean Riley, who often accompanied the youth group on outings.

Juli thought about how the kids seldom seemed to relate to them as grown-ups, and how they didn't act "chaperonish." Juli grinned at her new word.

After dinner and cleanup, they gathered on the carpet in front of a blazing fire. The well-sealed log walls gave a cozy feeling of long ago and far away. "It's like something out of 'Little House on the Prairie,' " Ashley murmured in Juli's ear.

"Do you like it?" Juli held her breath.

"No." The word came out flat, shocking.

Every hope for drawing the girl from Cove into their youth group crashed. Only a few times in Juli's life had she been so bitterly disappointed. It must have shown in her face, for Ashley grabbed her arm and said, "Don't look like it's the end of the world. I said I don't like it because I *love* it!"

It took a few moments for Juli to rebound. When she did, she wanted to jump up and yell, "Yes!" But she knew better. Making Ashley the center of attention would not be smart. Juli contented herself with smiling and saying, "That's good to hear." She glanced around the circle of faces. "We probably won't get a column out of this, except for yours and Jessica's, but I'm really glad you came."

"Who could resist your sales pitch?" Ashley muttered.

Her prickly answer couldn't keep Juli from secretly rejoicing. She also noticed how attentively Ashley listened when Kareem gave a prayer at bedtime after the singing. Juli gave silent thanks and let her imagination run. Ashley Peterson's admission that she loved something meant a lot. It also revealed that she was beginning to fit into the group who had welcomed and accepted her so readily.

Between dinner and devotions, Juli spread out her sleeping bag between Shannon's and Ashley's, with her cocolumnist next to Jessica's bed. The other girls took up most of the space in between them and Christy—a small, blue-eyed cocoon on the floor beside Jasmine.

The youngest member of the retreat was also first into bed. She asked Jessica with the innocent curiosity of childhood, "Why don't your legs go?"

Chattering ceased. Ashley glared at Christy. Only Jessica acted natural. She made a face and said, "I wish I knew. So do the doctors."

"Really?" Encouraged by the older girl's nod, Christy went on. "Why don't the doctors know? Did your legs used to work?"

Jessica nodded.

"Why don't they now?" Christy stopped. She added in a small voice, "Am I asking too many questions? Dave said not to be a pest."

"I don't mind." Jessica smiled at the little girl and swiftly glanced at the others. "Most of you already know my father and I were in a car crash a couple of years ago. He died. My spine was hurt."

Christy's eyes opened wide. "Ohhh." One hand flew to her mouth. A murmur of sympathy ran through the room.

"It's all right. I still miss him, but it's getting easier." Jessica's eyes misted.

"Have you been in a wheelchair ever since?" Jasmine softly asked.

She shook her head. "Yes, but not from the injury." The shadow came back to her face. "The specialists say my body healed, but the shock of losing Dad did something to my mind. It isn't sending the right signals to my legs so that I can walk yet." She lifted her chin and a brave smile tilted her lips up. Faith rang in her voice. "I believe it will happen. One of these days, you'll see me without my wheelchair. I'll challenge you all to a race, and I'll win, too!"

"I'll cheer for you, Jessica," Christy promised.

"We all will," Jasmine said. "Now, lights out, girls. Tomorrow is going to be a long and busy day."

After a few giggles and a little whispering, the room became quiet. Juli's heart ached. She prayed Jessica's faith would be answered. If nothing were wrong physically, surely God would help Jessica's mind and body coordinate. The name Jessica means "wealthy." Juli and Shannon had looked it up after meeting the Carrs. Some of the greatest wealth God could give Jessica would be the use of her legs.

Juli's active brain traveled on. She thought of Emily Carr, courageous enough to let her daughter attempt hard things. "Emily" means "industrious." How hard she must have fought to bring Jessica out of bitterness to the confident belief that one day she would abandon her wheelchair and walk again.

A slight nudge from Ashley made Juli turn on her side to face her.

"Why would your God make Mr. Carr die and take away the use of Jessica's legs?" Ashley fiercely whispered.

"He didn't," Juli whispered back. "A car wreck did that."

After a long time, Ashley nudged her again. "Couldn't God have changed things?" She must have felt Juli nod, for she quickly said, "Why didn't He?"

A dozen answers flitted through Juli's mind. None fit. She whispered, "I don't know why God steps in and changes some situations but lets others stand." She took a deep breath. "No one knows except Him. That's why He is God."

Ashley lay still for such a long time, Juli thought she had fallen asleep. Then she said in a voice so low Juli had to strain to hear it, "Thanks for being honest." She turned over, ending the conversation.

Juli took comfort in the fact Ashley hadn't scoffed. There had been anger in her question because of Jessica, but Juli suspected Ashley really wanted to know. Why hadn't the other girl been more bitter, more unyielding? Perhaps Jessica's faith and trust were preaching a finer sermon than any Ashley could hear from the pulpit. *I hope so, God.* Juli smiled, yawned, and fell asleep.

"Dishes are done," Dave sang out the next morning shortly after breakfast. "Thanks for helping with K.P., Jessica. What are you going to do now that you've peeled, sliced, and diced a mountain of vegetables for soup?"

She cocked her bright brown head. "Ashley and I are going to bake a cake while some of the guys get a sled run ready. She doesn't ski." Flags of color waved in Jessica's cheeks. "It's been a long time since I went tobogganing."

Juli caught Dave's warning glance above Jessica's head. She bit her tongue. When would she learn the disabled girl knew what she could and couldn't do? As responsible as she appeared, Jessica would never put herself in danger by acting foolish. Or through trying to impress others by being who she wasn't.

Juli secretly admitted she couldn't say the same for herself all the time. She occasionally did something world-class dumb in order to make an impression. She could learn a lot from Jessica.

The morning flew by on wings of happiness. By noon, intense blue gave way to a paler sky. Nothing in the weather forecast had indicated anything unusual, so the group ignored the sky, devoured hot soup and sandwiches, and went back outdoors. The nonskiers took good care of Jessica. They tucked her safely onto a long sled, swooshed down the packed hill, and trudged back with her to go down again. Amy, Carlos, and others practiced skiing on a gentle slope.

"Let's find a harder ski run than the ones we used this morning," Dave suggested. "They're fine for beginners, but not much of a challenge."

"Good idea," Juli enthusiastically agreed. Shannon nodded. Dave grabbed his ski poles. Kareem decided to go with them. Ted admitted the beginner slopes were more his speed, so he stayed behind. The others found what looked like the perfect run. Kareem insisted on testing it first. He came back smiling. "Let's go!"

"Better than flying!" Juli said to Dave after an exhilarating run and a hard climb back to the top. She prepared to go again. Shannon held one ski upright for balance while she knelt to check a boot. Her patterned scarf made a bright spot of color against her dark green ski suit.

Movement to Juli's left caught her attention. She riveted her gaze on the spot, unable to trust her own eyes.

A pale, ghostlike face peered at her and her friends from behind a heavily drifted tree branch, bent low from its burden of white.

CHAPTER 9

Why would anyone be lurking at the top of a hill out here, miles from anywhere? Juli wondered. Impossible! *Oh, yeah?* a little voice inside her taunted. *Then how come your heart is pounding like a bass drum?* The face disappeared. The heavy thud of her heartbeat continued.

Shannon looked up from her kneeling position. "What's wrong? You look like you just saw a ghost." Her merry laugh showed how little she believed it.

"I did. I mean, not a ghost exactly, but someone was watching us from behind that tree," Juli whispered. She pointed to the tree.

"I don't see anyone. Are you sure it wasn't just—"

The crunch of snow interrupted. The four persons staring at the snow-laden tree whipped around. Shannon gasped and clutched her upright ski. Kareem and Dave froze. Fear dried Juli's mouth. This couldn't be happening.

It was. Winter sunlight reflected on the shaved heads of two men who came toward them. Their expressionless faces held less warmth than the frozen ponds Juli and her friends skated on near Bellingham. Military surplus clothing that normally blended into the woods and camouflaged its wearers, showed stark and frightening against the white world in which they stood. Juli recognized the assault weapons they carried from seeing such guns on TV newscasts.

The malice and contempt in the men's eyes when they glared at Kareem sent fresh terror through Juli. Words rushed to her stunned brain. Skinheads. White supremacists. Neo-Nazis. A black cloud of danger hovered over her beloved youth leader. She marveled at his control when he took a step forward and said pleasantly, "Hello. May we help you?"

A burst of profanity followed, so vile it made the girls cringe. Dave growled low in his throat and started forward. Juli clutched his arm in a grasp of steel. Her searching gaze had detected three more similarly dressed people, partially concealed by gigantic tree branches that drooped to the ground. She felt a false move might bring tragedy. What did the strangers want, anyway? Just to bully someone?

Juli's keen ears caught the distant shouts of her friends sledding and building snow figures near the log house. They couldn't know of the drama being played out on the otherwise peaceful slopes above them. Juli closed her eyes tightly. No help would come from below. It must come from above. *Please, God, help us.* She saw Shannon's pale lips moving and realized her friend was also praying. It brought a tiny amount of comfort, but her spine was still one big icicle.

It felt like hours before the man acting as leader answered Kareem, but Juli knew just a few seconds had passed. The unwelcome visitor raised his fist and said in a deadly, hate-driven voice, "The only way you and your black-loving friends can help is by going back to Africa. The sooner you learn that real Americans don't want you here—you and your kind—and you leave, the better off we'll all be."

Juli swallowed hard. The leader's raw hatred sickened her. So did the quick mutter of agreement from the second visible man. Juli had faced danger before, but never like this. A feeling of absolute evil poisoned the crisp mountain air.

Kareem didn't even raise his voice. "I'm sorry you feel that way. America should be big enough—"

"Shut up!" The second man lunged forward, weapon ready.

A curt command from the leader stopped him. Shannon gave a cry of distress. She tried to muffle it with her hands but was too late. The second man scowled at her. "Who are you and what are you looking at? Didn't your mother teach you better than to stare?"

It sounded so bizarre coming from him that Juli had to cover her explosion of nervous laughter with a fit of hard coughing.

If looks really could kill, she'd have died on the spot. Her hope of distracting the man from Shannon faded. The man withered Juli with a glance, then demanded of her friend, "Well? Who are you?"

"Shannon Riley." She scrambled to her feet, her face

the color of ashes. "My mother's for bein' dead." The Irish brogue brought on by fear made the word "mother" sound more like "mither."

He didn't move a muscle. "You're Irish."

The blunt accusation sent Juli's brain scrambling. Did white supremacists hate Irish people, as well as Jews, African-Americans, Asians, and others?

Shannon licked her dry lips. Juli expected a nod or a meek "Yes." Instead, Shannon quietly said, "I am." Her mouth dropped open in shock when he said, "They have the right idea over there: Kill off everyone who gets in the way. It cleans up the country for decent people."

Juli gave thanks that Shannon didn't argue. Now was not the time for her friend to take a stand about the so-called Irish holy war. The men also would never believe the explanation of Shannon's Rileyisms, if she unintentionally misquoted something that offended them.

The leader jerked his head toward Dave and Juli. "Who are you and what are you doing here with his kind?" He waved at Kareem.

Juli felt Dave's muscles tense. She gripped his arm even harder in warning.

"Dave Gilmore."

The seconds it took Dave to identify himself gave Juli time to think. If she used the name Kareem, it might enrage the men even more. "I'm Juli Scott. Mr. Thompson is our church youth group leader."

Their sneering expressions showed she had guessed wrong. So did the man's venom-dripping tone as he spat out, "*Mr.* Thompson!" He swore, and his light-blue eyes looked like frozen marbles. "So now they're trying to take over our churches! What do you—?"

Laughing voices broke into his tirade. Never had Ted Hilton's clownish face looked more welcome than when he yelled from partway up the path Juli and the others had made as they'd climbed to the top of the hill. "Day is dying in the west, east, south, and north," he bellowed. "Come on down. I'm hungry again. Besides, you've been gone so long, Carlos and Amy got concerned. I nobly volunteered to lead them to you." He motioned to the two figures clambering up the trail behind him. "Haven't you noticed how dark it's getting? Looks like more snow."

His last remark barely registered. Neither did the dull gray sky. Juli fixed her gaze on the trudging figures behind Ted. A fresh wave of horror threatened to buckle her knees. *Carlos and Amy must not come closer.* Who knew how these fanatics would react to seeing the blonde cheerleader with a Mexican-American! She wanted to shout "Go back!" The words stuck in her throat. That kind of challenge could set the intruders blazing like a match to dry kindling.

Dave called down the hill, "Thanks for reminding us. Time flies when you're having fun. Ready, everyone?" he added in a voice far too loud.

Juli turned back toward the two men. *Please, God, don't let them take what Dave said as a challenge. Will they try to stop us from leaving?*

"Get going," the leader snarled. "If you know what's good for you and your do-gooder Sunday school bunch, you'll keep your mouths shut." A few giant strides took him out of sight behind a tree where Juli knew another man waited. His companion cast a vicious glance at each of the skiers, then followed.

"Come on," Kareem urged. Sweat beaded on his face. "You first, Shannon. Juli next, then Dave. I'll bring up the rear."

"No way." Dave set his jaw. "What's to keep them from waiting until we're out of sight and picking you off with one of those assault weapons? You're in more danger than we are. The girls go first, then you. I come last."

"It's my responsibility," Kareem reminded. Dave stubbornly shook his head and refused to budge.

"Don't be for arguin' about it," Shannon cried. "Let's just go!" She scrambled into her skis and pulled her spruce green hood over her short dark hair.

Dave and Kareem looked ashamed. "You're right. Shove off. We'll be right behind you. Both of us," Kareem promised. "I doubt even hate groups like this will be bold enough for a killing with so many people nearby."

Fear lent wings to their skis. With Dave's gruesome suggestion ringing in her ears, Juli schussed down the slope a safe distance behind Shannon. Never had she been more conscious of her canary-yellow jacket. The color made her far more visible than any of the other three—the perfect target for a marksman far less accomplished than most men who armed themselves with assault rifles.

She tensed. Could they get to the bottom before a blast of gunfire shattered the falling dusk and destroyed lives? Another frantic prayer for help settled Juli down and she concentrated on her skiing. At the moment, she hated everything about the rush of cold air, the exhilarating feeling that came with the sport. Skiing for fun was wonderful. Racing downhill while expecting a hail of bullets to follow was a nightmare experience she'd never dreamed could happen.

Juli made it to the foot of the hill, shifted her body weight forward, skidded into a turn, and slid to a stop beside a shivering Shannon. They watched Dave and Kareem's powerful figures gather speed. How could a few short minutes feel like a lifetime? Juli sagged with relief when the other two reached the bottom, their matching parallel form far superior to hers, and stopped.

"Don't say anything to the others. At least not yet," Kareem warned. Shadows played over his face. "We'll hope and pray it won't be necessary to say anything at all." The flicker in his dark, brooding eyes did nothing to reassure Juli. Knowing that members of a hate group skulked on the mountainside with night coming on was enough to give her the creeps.

The glowing fire and warm welcome of the log house helped chase away some of her alarm. Yet even that comfort was denied when Jessica Carr unobtrusively motioned Juli aside. The younger girl's eyes looked bigger than the fat molasses cookies Mom sometimes made. "Something happened while you were gone, didn't it?" she said in a voice so low no one else could hear.

Juli tried not to show her shock at the unexpected question. "Why?"

"Kneel down and pretend you're looking at my nails.

Ashley gave me a manicure this afternoon when I got tired of being outdoors."

Juli obeyed. How could Jessica suspect anything about the ugly incident? Even Ted hadn't been close enough to notice anything unusual.

"I sent Ashley back outside," Jessica whispered. "That's when I heard it."

Juli's nerves screamed. "Heard what?"

"Shh. I flipped on the radio to get the weather. The announcer said there's a group of crazies somewhere between Tacoma and Mount Rainier." She raised her voice and said for the benefit of anyone who might be observing them, "If Ashley ever wants a second career, she can go into the beauty business."

Under cover of the general laughter and teasing of an obviously pleased Ashley, Jessica informed Juli, "The police are looking for five men with shaved heads, assault weapons, and combat-type clothes who are headed this way. They're suspects in the beating of a Tacoma businessman who spoke out against terrorist groups." Her intelligent gaze never left Juli's face. "Ted said you were gone a long time. When you came in, Shannon huddled by the fire. You girls, Kareem, and Dave are putting on an act. You're good, but not good enough."

The corners of her mouth turned down. "I should know! I did it plenty before I started believing things would get better." She hastily added, "I did it for Mom."

Now what? Juli wondered. Kareem had asked for secrecy, but he hadn't counted on Jessica getting the newscast. Before long, everyone would know the men the police called crazies could be close by. Would the youth group panic if they learned some of their own people had been detained by what must be those very men?

After a long moment, Juli said, "I don't have the right to tell you anything, Jessica, except that I have to talk with Kareem. Okay?"

"Sure." The other girl gave a thumbs-up sign. "I won't say anything or ask questions." She made a zipping motion with fingers across her lips.

Juli eyed the crowd. "Good. Now if I can just get to Kareem!"

It proved impossible. Jasmine had laughingly laid claim to her husband for help with a special song she wanted to teach the group. Their blended voices came from the upstairs bedroom. What should Juli do now?

"Are you okay?" Dave asked from behind her.

Juli turned. "Not really. I need to tell Kareem something but I don't dare pry him away from his wife." She tried to sound casual and failed miserably.

"If it's about the goons we met on the hill, he already knows. Don't say anything, but Ted came inside for a drink of water and overhead the news flash Jessica picked up on the radio. He didn't let on, even to her."

"Has Kareem reported that the men are or were here?"

Dave's blue eyes beneath his short, light-brown hair looked troubled. "Don't panic, but the phone's dead. The line could be down. Or it could have been cut for insurance." He shrugged. "We can't find out tonight. I suggested packing us all into the bus and heading for home. Kareem said no. Those guys know they've been seen.

They may make tracks. We also may be safer here than going down the winding mountain road in the dark."

"You mean because it's so narrow?"

"That and because there are just too many places where we have to slow down to turn corners. Every one of them offers excellent cover for someone who wants to stop the bus and—"

"And take hostages," she finished for him. "Or the bus. Or both." The idea made her skin crawl. Had a group ever been more vulnerable? Kareem and Jasmine Thompson plus Carlos Ramirez, all of them guilty of the "crime" of being born with a skin color that offended hate groups. Christy Gilmore, nine years old. Jessica Carr, confined to a wheelchair.

"Okay, fellow P.I. Let's see what we have." Dave managed a grin. "It doesn't make sense for men on the run to get involved with a church youth group."

"It also didn't make sense for them to confront us," Juli told him.

"There's a good chance they wouldn't have bothered if Kareem had been white," Dave said quietly. "We used most of our breath for climbing when we came back up after our first trip downhill. Besides, snow muffles voices. The creeps may not have realized anyone was around until they spotted us."

Juli wasn't completely convinced. "That's a lot of ifs and maybes."

"I know, but it's the best we have. Look on the bright side. Your dad must know the situation, along with Andrew and Mary Payne and the rest of the world. If there's the slightest danger, help is already on the way."

Juli clung to the encouraging thought all through games and dishes, singing and sharing. In the glow of the dying fire, several of the kids told about times that they felt God had been with them. None made a big deal of it or got preachy. They simply shared stories involving their Friend.

Juli saw Ashley Peterson brush her eyes after Shannon's touching story of escaping from a cult. "The only way I could shut out the brainwashing was to repeat Psalm 23:4—'I will fear no evil: for thou art with me'—over and over," Shannon said. "Those ten words kept me going." She smiled. "And here I am!"

"For which we are glad," Ted remarked into the hush that followed her story. His eyes twinkled. "Can anyone here imagine a world without Rileyisms?" The emotion-charged moment passed in a burst of laughter.

Ashley's thoughtfulness did not. Later she whispered to Juli, "It's funny how everyone can be thoughtful one minute and laughing the next. Doesn't God mind? I always thought that if there really were a God, He'd be pretty serious."

"Do you really think the God who put horns on rhinoceroses and humps on camels doesn't enjoy a good laugh?" Juli demanded.

"Good point." Ashley giggled. "Good night. I can't wait until tomorrow."

Not me, Juli thought. *Right now, I feel safe. Too bad the tomorrows don't come with money-back guarantees that everything will be all right.*

CHAPTER 10

Weary from the long day of fresh air and exercise, the church youth group and their leaders slept heavily in the snug log house. They slept when the first large snowflakes began falling, gathering companions on their way down. They slept while a thick white blanket deepened on the ground, trees, roof, and bus. They didn't stir when a wind came up and blew the snow into great drifts. No one awakened until a heavy blast just after daybreak tore around the corners of the house and rattled windows.

Christy Gilmore sat up. "What's that?" Tousled light-brown hair around her sleep-filled blue eyes made her look more like Dave than ever.

"Sounds like a storm," Juli answered, pulling her sleeping bag closer under her chin.

"Brr! It's freezing in here. What happened to the heat?"

A tap at the bedroom door brought a chorus of, "Hello. What's happening?"

Kareem Thompson's crisp reply woke everyone who

was not yet conscious. "We're in the middle of a blizzard. The outdoor thermometer is holding steady at just over twenty degrees, and we've lost our electrical power. The boys are building a roaring fire in the fireplace. I'll leave your door partly open and see if we can get some heat into your boudoir." His rich laugh sounded encouraging. "Stay in bed until we get rid of the chill, then climb into your woollies."

"Gladly," Juli mumbled before sliding further down in her cozy nest.

"A real blizzard?" Christy squealed. She bounded from bed to the window, looking ridiculously small in her animal-patterned, footed pajamas. She excitedly swept the curtain aside with one hand and pressed her nose to the frosted glass.

Juli grinned. She used to do the same thing, especially when the first snow came. She still remembered the wonder of looking out into a white world.

Christy's whoop of delight brought answering smiles. They died when the little girl cried, "The snow is almost up to the windowsill. This is so cool!" She turned from the window and danced up and down. "We're trapped by the snow. We'll have to stay here forever and ever!"

"That long?" Jasmine teased, even though a worried look came to her eyes.

"I hope so." Christy shivered and wrapped her arms around herself, continuing to stare out the window.

"I don't," Shannon whispered to Juli. "Not with those creeps around. I wonder how they survived the storm?"

"They're trained in survival." Juli cast a concerned

look toward the window. "I'm not sure even they could handle this, though. It came so suddenly!"

"Come back to bed," Jasmine told Christy. "Here. Crawl in with me."

The child tore herself away from the fascination with a changed world. "Okay." She hopped across the room on one foot, skillfully avoiding stepping on the girls who were still snuggled in their beds on the floor.

Juli caught the concern in Ashley's eyes when she quietly asked Jessica, "Will you be all right?"

Laughter spilled from the girl in the twin bed. It warmed the chilly room. "Of course. I've always secretly wanted to be snowbound. I had a teacher who quoted the same poem every time it snowed." She deepened her voice to sound teacherish. "James Russell Lowell wrote 'The First Snow-Fall' well over a hundred years ago, class. Just think of it! His words are as appropriate now as in 1849. Close your eyes and picture what he describes. We're fortunate to live in Washington State where we can see at least some snow practically every winter. Listen." Jessica began to quote. Juli closed her eyes.

"The snow had begun in the gloaming,
And busily all the night
Had been heaping field and highway
With a silence deep and white.
Every pine and fir and hemlock
Wore ermine too dear for an earl,
And the poorest twig on the elm-tree
Was ridged inch-deep with pearl."

"What's the gloaming and ermine and an earl?" Christy piped up.

Jessica didn't seem to mind. Her brown eyes sparkled when she explained, "That's what we asked our teacher. She said gloaming comes at the end of day—we usually call it dusk or twilight. Ermine is an animal that has white fur in winter. An earl is an important person in England and some other countries." She went on with the poem, carefully omitting sad parts about the death of a child that would disturb Christy. She finished with little Mabel asking who made it snow, and the father's answer,

> *"And again to the child I whispered,*
> *'The snow that husheth all,*
> *Darling, the merciful Father*
> *Alone can make it fall!'* "

"I know what hush means," Christy crowed. "It's be still. Keep quiet. That's what Dave tells me when I ask too many questions." She waved a testing finger in the air while the others laughed. "Hey, it's getting warmer. Can we get up?"

"Yes, but in ones and twos," Jasmine told her. "We can't all crowd into the bathroom at one time." Her soft laugh brought sympathetic smiles. "Not that we'll be staying long! Who's first to wash up in cold water? Molly? Amy?"

Molly Bowen groaned and burrowed deeper into her sleeping bag. "I don't think so. I'll play groundhog and stay in bed until spring or the electricity comes back on, whichever is first."

"Thanks, but no thanks," Amy said. "A cold water bath is too much."

"You're all saved from such a horrible fate," Kareem called from the hallway. "The boys and I heated water in a big kettle in the fireplace. Use it sparingly, cool it to lukewarm, and you'll have enough for one washbowl apiece."

Ashley sat up. "I'll be brave and go first." She stood and stretched. "Isn't it funny? We'd have complained like crazy if Kareem had told us at first we only got a washbowl of lukewarm water to bathe in." She grinned. "After Jasmine said we'd be washing up in cold water, that washbowl apiece sounds fantastic!" She abruptly changed subjects. "Hey, Juli, maybe we'll get another column out of this retreat after all. Wonder if our editor would approve a comparison article? You know, the way people today survive storms compared with the olden days."

"Sounds great." Juli peered through the spot on the window Christy had rubbed clear. Heavy snow still fell. "By the time we get back to Bellingham, we may have more material than we need," she said soberly.

Yet even the seriousness of their situation couldn't dampen the holiday mood of the snowbound group. Everyone pitched in to help stay "reasonably clean, reasonably warm, and reasonably fed," as Ted jokingly put it. Kareem and the boys went outside following breakfast. Hot instant cocoa was made with water heated in the fireplace, and slightly scorched bread toasted on a long fork over the fire. Laughing voices and the steady *swish-thud, swish-thud* of busy shovels making paths echoed in the still air. Snow continued to steadily fall. The group could take no chances. The large supply of neatly stacked firewood might not hold out. Without electricity or phone service, the group had no way to get radio news and learn how widespread the storm was. A nearby dead tree would provide extra fuel, but there must be a broad trail between it and the log house.

"Hope for an early rescue is foolish," Dave privately told Juli when he shrugged into his silver and black ski jacket before going outdoors.

"I know. Dad, the Paynes, even a helicopter can't get through to us until this blizzard ends." She stared into his concerned face and whispered, "Y–you don't think those men died in the storm do you?"

"I hope not." Dave zipped his jacket. "They're pretty good at finding shelter."

His words gave her little comfort. Finding shelter in such a blizzard seemed beyond belief even for groups trained in survival methods.

"I don't want to alarm you," Kareem had told his charges while they ate, "but a freak storm like this can cripple all of Western Washington. It's both early and came without warning. It will take time for people to dig out. No way will the church bus plow through this amount of snow. Even if it did, the wind may have brought trees down across the road."

His serious tone got through even to Christy. She huddled close to Dave. "Are we going to starve?" she asked in her direct way. "There's lots of us and we ate 'most everything yesterday, 'cause we thought we were going home today."

"Are you kidding?" Her big brother gave her a hug. "Didn't you see all the food in the cupboards? Kareem and Jasmine's friends keep this place well stocked." He tickled Christy.

She giggled and squirmed free. "Did God tell your friends to buy lots of food so it would be here for us?" she asked the Thompsons.

Jasmine smiled at the earnest little girl. "He certainly knew we'd need it, didn't He?" She held out her hand. "Let's form a ways and means committee, girls. Christy, I'll give you a pencil and some paper. Ashley, you call out what food is in the cupboards and how much of each item. Christy will make a list for us. Deciding on menus will be a real challenge. We don't know how long we may have to cook in the fireplace."

Christy looked delighted with her responsibility, and Jasmine went on with her assignments. "Jessica, someone has to feed the fire. That will be you. Keep a steady blaze. It's our only source of heat."

"All right, only someone needs to bring in more wood." She grinned impishly. "I could handle it, but getting my wheelchair in and out so many times would let in more cold than we want!"

"What about the rest of us?" Shannon asked when they stopped laughing.

"Some of you make sure our fire-keeper is well supplied with wood. The rest can carry wood to the house after Kareem and the boys cut and split it. Exercise will warm you."

A flash of understanding came to Juli. Jessica couldn't exercise her legs. That's why Jasmine had given her an important job but one she could do and still stay warm. *Please, God, don't let Jessica suffer from our being stuck here. She's so special. Please help Emily and the rest of our folks not be too worried.* Juli paused in her silent prayer, then felt compelled to add, *And please don't let those men die. Even though they do awful things, don't let them die.*

Shannon's call from the doorway interrupted Juli's silent prayer. "Come on, slowpoke. There's wood to be carried."

"Right." Juli stepped outside the log house into a white, white world. Shannon, Molly, Amy, and the rest of the wood-carrying detail followed.

Shannon motioned toward a cluster of figures by the half-buried bus. "I wonder what's happening." She hurried down the trail the boys had cleared, with Juli and the other girls right behind her. They reached Kareem and the boys, all of whom stood staring at the open door of the bus. Something moved inside it.

The tramp of feet down the aisle turned Juli's heart to lead. Five grim-faced, unshaven men marched down the steps carrying their assault weapons.

A ripple of shock went through the youth group. Amy's mittened hand flew to her mouth and cut a scream in half.

"Not a bad hotel you have here," the leader of the party

said. His words fell like enormous pellets of hail, cutting and dangerous.

For the second time, Juli marveled at Kareem Thompson's iron control. His jaw set in a firm line, he answered in an even voice, "Glad you used it for shelter. It's pretty crowded in the house. Making breakfast in a fireplace isn't easy, but we can offer hot cocoa and toast."

Someone gulped. Juli suspected it came from shock. Except for Kareem, who had witnessed some pretty terrible things as a child in Africa, none of the church bunch had ever seen people armed like this except on TV or in the movies.

Surprise and something impossible to identify sprang to the men's faces. The leader took a step forward. Kareem's quiet voice halted him. "You won't need your weapons."

"Oh, yeah?" A scowl replaced the flicker of surprise that had made the unexpected breakfast guests more human for a moment. "If you think we're leaving them in the bus, think again, black man. How stupid can you get?"

Juli bit her lips to keep from screaming. How could Kareem remain so calm? Dumfounded, she heard the youth leader say, "Black I am. I may also be stupid, but not stupid enough to allow any of my group to touch your weapons. Are you ready for breakfast?"

Juli scarcely dared breathe. If miracles came in small doses, the grudging respect in the pale blue eyes of the racist leader was one of them. He grunted. "Yeah, but our weapons go with us."

Kareem shrugged as if to say he'd done his best. "Please don't frighten my wife and the little girl inside," he requested. "If you'll follow me, please. Group, finish shoveling a path to the snag. Look for downed branches sticking up through the snow. Don't try anything stupid, like starting to cut down the snag before I come back."

Juli's rapid glance traveled from face to face. Each showed the command not to do anything stupid related to much more than cutting down a snag. Shannon put it into words after Kareem led the five men into the house. "Kareem was for warnin' us not to be rushin' in where the devil fears to go."

Strained nerves relaxed into laughter. "Shh!" Juli hissed, with a lightning look at the house. "They mustn't think we're laughing at them."

"They might laugh if they heard Shannon's translation of 'fools rush in where angels fear to tread.' " Dave chuckled. "We won't take chances, though." He raised a questioning eyebrow at Juli. "We may as well explain about yesterday."

"What happened yesterday?" John Foster demanded. Ted Hilton looked wise.

Dave filled them in. "I don't think we are in real danger, but we can't be sure. If we are, Kareem and Carlos will be prime targets. It's probably smart for you to keep a low profile and stay away from Amy," he told the dark-haired boy. "Hate groups are radically opposed to friendship between races." When Carlos stubbornly set his mouth, Dave added, "It's not just you. Amy could be in danger, too."

Carlos nodded, but didn't reply.

Dave obviously wasn't finished. Juli dreaded what

she suspected was coming.

The tall boy scuffed his boots in the snow. "This storm can't last forever. Until it's over, we'll probably be stuck with our uninvited guests. The best thing we can do is make the best of it, if there is a best. And *not* make waves."

CHAPTER 11

Don't make waves. Dave Gilmore's warning beat into Juli's brain until she thought she would go mad. She recognized the wisdom of his advice. She admitted that no other choice lay open to the youth group. Yet every passing hour made it harder. A dozen times she started to protest the way the five men treated Kareem and Jasmine Thompson. Never had she seen adults show such disrespect to other human beings. Juli secretly clenched her hands again and again. She hated the anger inside her. At the same time she longed to beat her fists against the intruders who ate their food and listened to every word anyone said. They also laughed when Kareem offered a blessing on the meals and kept up a running conversation during devotions that evening.

Shannon yanked Juli into the bathroom long enough to furiously say, "I'd like to tell the *spalpeens* who asked if my mother didn't teach me manners what their mothers taught them. They're ruder than if they'd been raised by pigs!"

Juli smothered her laughter in her towel. The youth group had already learned no one laughed at the intruders. Ted made an innocent joke to lighten the dark mood that had fallen over the occupants of the log house, and one of the men shook his fist and told him to shut up. Juli believed he'd have decked Ted, if the leader of the unwelcome visitors hadn't stepped between them.

Too keyed up to sleep that night, Juli's forehead wrinkled. Something about the leader set him apart from the others. Was it his unsmiling authority? She shook her head. No, a difference she couldn't explain surrounded the tall man. She'd have expected him to stay out of the situation between his man and Ted. Why hadn't he? If she could figure it out, she might have a clue about the best way to endure living in the same cabin until the storm ended and help came.

Juli closed her eyes and concentrated. Her brain replayed each event since the strangers stepped down from the church bus. She quickly skipped over the tense moments until Kareem led the five men into the house for breakfast. After Dave warned those huddled together not to make waves, he led the wood detail in search of downed branches. Juli hesitated.

"Coming?" he'd called.

She put gloved fingers to her lips. "Shh. In a minute."

Dave's eyebrows had shot up and he'd given her one of his looks. The kind that silently shouted for her not to do anything stupid. She took a step toward him and the others, then stopped. The burning desire to go inside and see what was happening proved stronger than Dave's warning look. Inside the cabin, the Thompsons, Ashley, Christy, and Jessica faced five dangerous men. They would be powerless against those trained in military tactics, should trouble arise.

So what can you do? the little voice inside that often challenged and mocked her demanded. "Be there," Juli said under her breath.

Ha! You don't even have an excuse, let alone a reason, for going back indoors.

Juli gritted her teeth. "That's what you think." She pulled off a warmly lined glove and tossed it to one side. "I can ask if I dropped my glove before I came out. It's not a lie. I won't say I dropped it, just ask if I did." She plotted her movements, then waited for a time to put them into action. She also put the time to good use by asking for God's help and protection.

Juli slowly turned the doorknob with her bare right hand. A wave of warmth from the fireplace hit her chilly face. Ten heads turned toward her. Ten pairs of eyes stared at her. Juli's courage began to melt. "Uh, did I drop one of my mittens in here?" she stammered.

No one replied. The strangers glared like she'd crawled out from under a rock.

"What's wrong?" she blurted out.

Christy Gilmore ran to her, blonde ponytail swinging. "I asked the men why they dressed so funny. He told me to shut up." She pointed an accusing finger at the man who had threatened Ted earlier.

Juli's heart jumped to her throat. Why didn't someone speak? The creeping feeling that it wouldn't matter what anyone said, especially the Thompsons, hit her. The most innocent words might flame the sparks of hatred in the room into a raging fire. If only Christy would keep still! Juli put her arm around the child.

Her movement didn't help or quiet Christy. The child's blue gaze traveled from face to face and landed on the leader's. "Why do you have guns? My daddy says guns do bad things."

Did the man wince, or was it Juli's imagination?

"Sometimes guns do good things," he curtly told Christy. "We use them to help make our country a good place for little girls like you."

She stared at him with eyes round as blue dinner plates. "That's funny. Do you have a little girl? My daddy says—"

Juli found her voice. "Climb into warm clothes and come help us drag in branches, will you please, Christy? Jessica is going to need a lot of wood. Besides, we might see a rabbit or deer or something."

Her diversion worked. Christy gave a squeal and clapped her hands before looking uncertain. "Ashley and I haven't finished our list."

"It doesn't matter," Jasmine said in her soft voice. "I need Ashley's help cooking breakfast for our visitors. You can finish making your food list later."

Christy ran to get ready. She came back wearing her hot-pink snowsuit and told Juli, "I looked and looked for your glove. Maybe you dropped it outside."

"Maybe." Juli managed a weak smile and hurried the little girl toward the door in an effort to get her outside before she blurted out anything else. Once in the yard, she suggested, "It's best not to ask the strangers too many questions. Some people don't like it."

Christy trotted beside her like a large, excited rose. "Why, Juli?"

"They just don't." Dumb answer, but the best she could come up with just then.

Christy gave a sigh. It sounded as though it began at her toes and gathered strength all the way up. "Big people always say that when they don't want to answer. When I grow up, I'm never going to say it. Or 'You'll understand when you get older,' either. That's what Dave always tells me. Why doesn't he 'splain things that I want to know?"

"Some things are hard to explain," Juli told her. "Even big people don't always understand."

Christy's mittened hand slipped into hers. "I like you, Juli." An impish smile broke out on her pixie face. "My brother does, too!" She danced up and down. Her gaze lit on something on the snow. "Here's your glove. You didn't lose it after all." She broke free and ran down the trail the boys had shoveled.

"What did you learn, Madam Super Sleuth?" Dave had asked a little later when Christy moved out of hearing.

"We need to keep your sister as far away from our not-so-honored guests as possible," Juli grimly said. Tongues of fear licked at her. "Some of her questions aren't any more welcome than the jerks who've moved in with us."

"You said it," Dave admitted. He cast a worried glance at the snow-clogged sky. "Help can't get through in this stuff, and we can't get out. It's too cold for the men to sleep in the bus tonight. I'd guess the only reason they did last night is because they had no idea how many people were in the house."

His guess proved correct. When early darkness fell, the five men remained with the church group, but definitely not part of it. They accepted food and shelter without a word of thanks to either God or those who provided it. They also kept their weapons close by, even after night fell and bedtime came. Not a single eye blinked when Kareem asked, "Since you'll be sleeping in front of the fireplace, do you mind keeping it stoked? Or shall I come down and tend it?"

Juli could almost see the wheels in the leader's mind going around. Hating nonwhites as the group did, no way would they trust an African-American among them in the dead of night. Their warped minds would certainly feel it a trick for Kareem to get his hands on one of the assault weapons.

After a long, thoughtful pause the leader said, "We'll do it. You stay where you belong and don't go sneaking around."

For the hundredth time since the invasion by the strangers, Juli had wondered how her youth leader could stay so cool. His simple questions and statements showed no offense. She couldn't say the same for herself. Juli knew better than to allow even a single word to escape her tightly locked lips. With it would come anger and bitterness. Kareem's—and God's—method of turning the other cheek and treating enemies well was a far better and safer way to blunt danger.

Now she turned restlessly in her sleeping bag, her thoughts continuing to swirl. If only she could pinpoint what it was about the leader. . . She fell asleep feeling she hovered right on the edge of something vitally important, but still was unable to name it.

Monday morning arrived with another downpour of snow. This time four of the invaders joined Kareem and the boys on the wood detail. The leader ordered the girls to stay inside. "I'll keep them company." A meaningful nod toward his weapon warned men and boys not to try anything.

Juli appointed herself a one-person committee to keep Christy away from him. He seemed to hold a horrid fascination for the youngest of the party. In turn, the leader . . .a tingle went through Juli. That was it, the difference that separated the leader from his men. Tough and determined, his expression when he glanced at Christy showed a faint hint of softness. Deeply buried beneath the crust of hatred lay a spark that showed the white supremacist leader had some good inside.

Could he be reached through that spark? Juli slowly shook her head. Using Christy to soften the leader might prove fatal. The little girl showed too much curiosity. She was also far too unpredictable. Not even Dave knew how his sister's mind worked or what she'd come up with next. All day, Juli kept Christy busy. In the kitchen. In the bedroom. Outdoors to run off some of her energy. Hopefully, she'd be tired enough to fall asleep early. But what about the next day? And the next, if it continued snowing?

"One day at a time," Juli whispered. "Things can't get worse." Wrong. That same afternoon, three men dressed in camouflage uniforms and carrying assault weapons identical to those owned by the others marched out of the woods. They demanded they be taken in, sheltered, and fed!

The entire group held its breath. Finally, Kareem said, "I'm sorry, but we've barely enough food for those who are already here. Surely you have supplies and shelter? No one could survive these past two days without them."

With a rough oath, one of the new arrivals raised his weapon and lunged at the youth leader. "No black's gonna tell me what to do!" he yelled.

A voice colder than steel and twice as deadly commanded, "Put it down."

The attacker paused long enough to glare in the leader's direction. "Says who?" he insolently asked.

Juli held her breath. Not once in the endless hours they'd been trapped by the storm had anyone used a name. They didn't now, either. Before the leader spoke, a look of recognition crossed the newcomer's face. "You're—"

"Don't say it. Just back off." The leader's mouth closed in a tight seam. He jerked his head toward the door. "Outside, all of you."

Juli would have given her entire college savings to

know what was said in the conversation she could only observe from the snow-crowned window. Dave took advantage of it to whisper, "Stop staring and listen. The storm is letting up, but who knows for how long? Someone has to go for help. Tonight. It's our only chance. Tempers are already high. It's only a matter of time until this dynamite situation explodes and someone gets hurt, maybe killed."

Lines that had not been in his face even that morning, deepened. "The way I figure, two persons have to go. If one doesn't make it, the other may. Ted can't ski well enough." He licked his lips. "We can. It will be dangerous. I don't know what they'll do to us if we get caught. It's up to us to see we don't."

A dozen objections rushed to Juli's mind. Each faded at memory of how close Kareem had come to being hurt. Her throat closed. All she could do was nod.

"Go out the window in your bedroom as soon as you think everyone's asleep," Dave ordered. "Whatever you do, *don't wear your yellow ski jacket!* Borrow Shannon's dark green outfit. Get it and get away without telling her, if you possibly can. The less she and the others know about our leaving, the better. For them, for us," he added half under his breath. "Uh-oh. The Gestapo's coming back inside." He gave her a tight-lipped smile and a quick, comforting hug. "Now is the time for all good P.I.s to come to the aid of their snow party."

Dave's light touch steadied her. So did the feel of his arm around her shoulders. Her mind raced. How could she ever sneak out from between Ashley and Shannon?

Should she make up a reason to move her bed closer to the window? She reluctantly gave up the idea. Changing after three nights might arouse suspicion, something she agreed with Dave they must not do. Having their absence discovered in the morning couldn't help being more than enough for the others to handle. Knowledge of the escape could be disastrous.

The eight men stamped back inside. "They stay," the leader announced. "Ration the food, if you have to. We're in this together. Either we all survive, or none of us will." His gaze strayed to Christy. Again Juli felt the blonde little girl held a key to the stern man who had taken them captive and taken command.

She clung to the thought and lay sleepless in her unzipped sleeping bag for an eternity. Ski boots under her pillow made a miserable lump. Her huge, cuddly fleece nightshirt felt tight over Shannon's ski suit. Juli had donned them in the bathroom earlier, counting on the dim glow of a kerosene lamp in the bedroom to conceal her extra bulk. A nervous giggle started. Juli smothered it in her pillow. Her friends gradually drifted into sleep. Juli waited. A grumbled conversation from the men in the living room ceased. Still she waited.

The dreaded moment came when she dared stay in the security of her sleeping bag no longer. Juli inched out and grabbed her boots. Ashley stirred. Juli froze. When the other girl breathed evenly again, Juli tiptoed to the window, thankful for the pitch-black darkness of the room. She put on her boots and worked the window open, desperately praying it would not scrape and betray her.

A lifetime later, she had a space wide enough to squirm through. The same careful closing followed. Freezing air pouring onto the sleeping girls meant certain betrayal. "Thank You, God," Juli breathed when she finished her task. She started to turn. She heard the scrunch of snow beneath boots, but too late. Cold sweat crawled beneath her clothing. She opened her mouth to scream for help.

A gloved hand seized her arm. Another covered her mouth, cutting off her cry.

CHAPTER 12

"Don't move or speak," a voice said close to Juli's ear.

Her knees buckled and she sagged against her captor. "Dave!"

The gloved hand fell away from her mouth. "Sorry I scared you. I couldn't take a chance on your thinking I was one of our guests."

He sounded so remorseful, Juli patted his arm before whispering, "It's okay. Where are our skis and poles? Is the crust heavy enough to hold us?"

"It has to be." He sounded grim. "It's freezing, so we should be all right. Come on. I took our gear from the porch and put it in the bus while waiting for you to sneak out the window." She saw him grin in the pale light of the stars. "I wonder if Romeo beneath Juliet's balcony felt the way I did tonight."

She followed him to the bus. "I doubt it. They only had two sets of angry parents, not a houseful of hate group members."

"Yeah." He disappeared into the vehicle looming above them like a snowbound blob. Juli shivered. She wouldn't relax until they reached a person who would help them, or at least send a message to someone who could. *Not even then,* she added to herself. She'd never be able to relax until the nightmare that began with their Saturday scare on top of the ski slope ended.

Dave crept out of the bus. "We won't put skis on until we get to unbroken snow. Let's go." He started down a shoveled trail. "Walk slowly and quietly. One of the first things people trained in survival do is develop their hearing. I'll bet those eight guys in the cabin have ears shaped like megaphones."

"Don't make me laugh," she pleaded. Her whisper didn't even reach the bus.

"Sorry." He led off. "Good thing there's no moon, at least so far."

Once they reached the end of the trail, they stopped to put on their skis. Juli's face tingled in the cold night air, and she tightened the strings of Shannon's parka hood. The frozen snow held, and they quickly moved out of sight of the cabin. They paused at the top of the mountain road that stretched white and empty before them. Dave pulled a flashlight from his pocket and cautiously shone the light down. "Do you think we can see enough by starlight?" he asked Juli. "I don't know how good the batteries are. I found it in a cupboard."

She waited until he turned the flashlight off and her eyes adjusted. "Maybe, but won't it slow us down terribly? It's going to be totally black where tree branches shadow the road." She peered ahead. "I'd guess Kareem and Jasmine's friends would make sure to keep new batteries in their flashlights. Look at how much food they had on hand."

"Yeah. We would have been fine until help came if it hadn't been for our guests," he said sourly. "You're right about the light, too. We can't take the chance of plowing into rocks or branches that are blocking the road." Dave turned the flashlight back on. "Ready?"

"Y–yes." Juli hoped he hadn't heard her gulp. Setting off in the middle of the night with no guarantee they'd succeed in getting help was bad enough. Dave did *not* need to know the senior member of Scott and Gilmore, P.I.s, had never been more frightened in her entire life! Yet she couldn't help asking, "Is there any chance we can reach help and get back without the others knowing?"

"I don't see how. Do you remember how far it is to the nearest cabin? Or seeing any signs of people in the few places we passed in the bus after we left the main road?"

"No. I wish I'd paid more attention."

"Why should you have, or any of us?" Dave replied. "We had no idea we'd run into fugitives up here where it seems so peaceful."

She heard the regret in his voice. "It isn't fair for people who choose rotten lifestyles to spoil things for the rest of us," she exploded.

"So who says life is fair?" He chuckled. "At least we'll have something to tell our grandkids. All about the night two brave—or is it reckless?—high school juniors rode off to the rescue. I mean, *skied* off to the rescue."

Juli felt a blush warm her cold face. She was glad Dave couldn't see it. His use of "our grandkids" didn't necessarily mean theirs together. Who knew what God had planned for either of them after high school and college? Juli grinned. She had enjoyed their time together since Dave asked her to be his girl *pro tem*—for the time being. Keeping things light made their friendship even more special.

"Ready?" Dave sounded impatient at having to ask a second time.

"Yes." Juli took a long breath of winter air. "One thing. We came together so that at least one of us can get through. If something, anything, happens, we stick with that plan." Instead of sounding firm, her voice came out wobbly.

"As in leaving the other person for the good of everyone," he hoarsely said. "If it happens, I hope it's you who has to go on, Juli. I'm not sure I could."

Understanding flowed through her. She'd never felt closer to Dave. "You must. Lives may depend on it." She reached out a gloved hand. "Remember, God will go with us." The words sounded a lot more confident than she felt. "He can also give us the strength to make hard choices."

"I know." He squeezed her hand and straightened his shoulders. "Let's go."

So began the strangest journey of Juli's short life. If she lived to be older than Mount Rainier, she'd never forget the fantastic trip down the winding mountain road. A sickly moon finally peered from beneath a cloud. It gave enough pale light for them to switch off the flashlight in open spaces. At other times, they relied on the single beam from the flashlight Dave carried. Twice they had to stop and remove downed branches from across the road.

"Things could be a lot worse," Dave muttered each time, taking the larger end. "It's a wonder whole trees aren't down."

Juli just grunted. She needed every ounce of energy to move her end of the branches. Hours of skiing and anxiety were draining her strength. Could she make it? *I have to, Lord,* she prayed. *Please help us.* She helped push the heavy branch to the side of the road, then staggered back to the middle and stood panting. If only morning would come! Her imagination turned every changing shadow into an evil grinning pursuer. Daylight would turn them back into what they really were: plain old shadows.

Juli refused to consider the fact that the coming of morning also increased their chance of being overtaken. Telltale ski tracks would help anyone following. So would the branch-free road. "I don't care," she whispered to herself. "This going back and forth between dark and light stretches is like something from a horror movie. Besides, when we can see better, Dave and I will be able to speed up."

"Did I mention that you're the world's best sport?" Dave asked between gasps.

His admiration made her smile. "No. You're not so bad yourself, Gilmore."

"Thanks, Juli." He waited until their breathing slowed. "Time to move."

"Do you want me to go first and break trail for a while?"

Dave shook his head. "Save your energy. You'll need it. I'm not trying to be macho, but I probably have more stamina than you do at this point."

Much as she hated to admit it, Juli knew he was right. She could feel signs of fatigue creeping over her. The benefits of breaking trail and allowing Dave to ease off for a time was outweighed by the drain on herself, which meant slowing him down. Would morning raise her drooping spirits as well as boost her physical ability to continue on? She hoped so. Setting her lips, she silently followed as closely in Dave's tracks as possible, praying for daylight to come soon.

In the log house far above, Ashley Peterson burrowed deep into her sleeping bag, hoping morning would never come. She clenched her teeth to keep them from chattering. Not from bodily cold, but from the chunk of ice her heart had become when she opened sleep-clouded eyes a long time earlier. A terrifying feeling of something wrong had settled over her, like the crushing weight of heavy snow on a rooftop. Ashley strained her ears but heard nothing. She carefully shifted position and listened again. What had disturbed her? Why?

No sound came from the living room where the intruders slept. No sound came from the girls' bedroom except one or two faint snores. Ashley sneaked her hand from her sleeping bag and reached to see if Juli had also awakened. She bit back a scream. Instead of the mound that showed her cocolumnist asleep and untroubled, Ashley's hand hit flat floor. She limply returned it to the warmth of her sleeping bag. *Don't be stupid,* she told herself. *Juli's gone to the bathroom.*

Ashley cautiously raised herself onto one elbow. Cold air rushed toward her. The window! Seconds later, the draft stopped. Ashley fell back. Waves of fear threatened to drown her. The empty bed, followed by the short rush of freezing air, could only mean one thing: Juli had slipped out the window.

Why? To meet Dave Gilmore?

Forget it. Juli wasn't like that. Even if she were, she and Dave had more sense than to prowl around while hate-filled men lay sleeping just down the hall, assault weapons right next to them. The only reason the girl Ashley once hated and envied would be crawling out the window in the dead of night was to go for help. Had she gone alone? Ashley doubted it. Juli and Dave must have cooked it up. She'd seen them talking earlier, both faces serious.

How could they? Ashley's mind protested. *If they're caught, something terrible may happen to them. Why not just wait until a rescue team or the Ski Patrol comes? Why would they risk their lives?*

Those were hard questions needing answers. But they weren't the only ones. Ever since she met the youth group and their smiling leaders, her belief that Christians were hypocrites had been challenged. Not one person at the retreat matched her stereotyped ideas. She had looked for signs that they were hypocrites and found none. Just the opposite. God and His Son Jesus were real to these people. It showed in everything they did. A person only had to look at the way Kareem and Jasmine Thompson treated the men who obviously hated and wanted to destroy them!

Longing to have what the others possessed stole into Ashley's troubled heart. Yet if there really were a kind and loving God, why didn't He heal Jessica? Even in the short time Ashley had known the girl in the wheelchair, she had learned to admire her tremendously. How could Jessica be so cheerful, so filled with the faith that she would walk again?

There is more than one way to be healed, a little voice inside Ashley whispered. *Doctors heal bodies. They cannot heal bitterness and hatred. Isn't the healing of a human spirit far greater than the healing of a body?*

Ashley jerked her mind back to Juli. Was it her belief in God that made her steal out a window and take the risk of punishment, in order to help others? Juli, and Dave if he had gone with her, hadn't run away. Dave would never do that with his sister here. Neither would Juli. She had gone for the sake of those she loved. Hot tears sprang to Ashley's eyes. She didn't know how she knew it was true, but if she, Ashley Peterson, had been the only one in danger, Juli and Dave would still have risked themselves to try and save her from their enemies.

Just like Jesus.

Ashley froze. Had someone spoken? No. The room remained still. The three words must have sprung from a dim corner of her brain, where they had been dropped and overlooked. Or ignored. Ashley winced. Every beat of her heart brought back things she had heard this weekend. Christians believed God loved the world He created so much that He sent His Only Son to save all those who would accept Him. When Jesus died on the cross, He took their punishment.

Ashley felt a tug-of-war begin inside her. Was it true? Why not? If two high school students from Bellingham, Washington cared enough to risk their lives for others, surely God would do even more. Would He have sent Jesus if Ashley were the only person on earth who needed saving? She had the feeling He would, but didn't know enough to be sure. Tomorrow, no, today, she'd ask Jessica. Or Shannon, or Kareem. If it really were true, how different life would be!

In the meantime, Juli and probably Dave were somewhere partway down the snowy mountain. "God, if You really are there, please help them," Ashley said into her pillow. She didn't know how to pray. She hoped the God Juli and the others believed in wouldn't care. This weekend had revealed a God of love and friendship, not a stern judge waiting to pounce on anyone who made a mistake.

A long time later, Ashley roused to the sound of yelling. She opened eyes she had believed would never fall asleep. Shannon sat on her sleeping bag, staring at Juli's empty bed on the floor between her and Ashley. Every trace of blue had faded from her eyes. They looked like stormy gray clouds. "Where is she?"

"Shh!"

"Is she all right?" Shannon's nails bit into Ashley's arm.

"Yes. I'll tell you later. *After* they question us, which they will," she grimly added. "Your face shows your feelings too easily. The less you or the others know, the better. Okay?"

A bit of color came back to Shannon's face. "Okay." It disappeared when the uniformed men ordered everyone present into the living room and the leader said, "One of my men found ski tracks. Two sets, made since it stopped snowing and frozen hard enough to bear the weight of skiers. Who is missing?"

No one replied.

His keen glance traveled over the group and stopped at Shannon. Ted Hilton put a protective arm around her. "Where is the girl who was with you on top of the ski slope Saturday?" he barked. "Juli Scott I think her name is."

"Yes." The Irish girl licked dry lips and slipped into brogue. "She was for bein' next to me when I fell asleep and gone when I woke just now."

"Are you telling me the truth?" His gaze bored into her. Ashley's heart bounced with thankfulness that Shannon could honestly nod yes.

"How about the rest of you? Did anyone see her go?"

Heads shook back and forth.

Ashley felt torn. She might not be a Christian—yet—but she hated a liar. Could she deliberately lie to save Juli and Dave? If pinned to the wall, maybe she could get away with half-truths. Before she made up her mind, the leader turned his gimlet eyes in her direction.

"You. Will you swear you neither saw nor heard Juli Scott leave the room?"

Ashley flung her head back. "I will." Relief shot through her at the wording of the question. She bit her lip to keep her expression from changing.

"Me, too," Christy Gilmore piped up in her childish voice, " 'cept Mommy says it's not nice to swear."

No one dared laugh. Not then. Not while the leader questioned Kareem and the boys, who knew nothing of Dave's disappearance. Especially not when they discovered Shannon Riley's hunter green ski pants and parka were also missing.

CHAPTER 13

Carlos Ramirez had succeeded in blending with the others and not attracting attention to himself, as Dave Gilmore had suggested. Then, without warning, the log house situation went from worse to impossible. Tuesday morning the leader stepped outside. As soon as he left, one of the three men who showed up the afternoon before, noticed the migrant workers' son. "Don't I know you?"

"I don't think so," Carlos quietly said. He sent a warning glance toward Amy Hilton, then Kareem Thompson, who took an impulsive step toward them.

"Oh, yeah?" The man continued to stare. His face turned ugly. He snapped his fingers. "Got it. You're the kid who took first prize in the Bellingham variety show and had his picture in the papers." His scowl deepened and he shook his fist in Carlos's direction. "Our guys should have won, not scum like you."

Our guys. Those two little words showed who had put the Hillcrest and Cove students up to dressing in Nazi uniforms and marching at the show. It also showed how closely members of hate groups kept in touch.

"I oughta beat the living daylights out of you," the man snarled.

Carlos gave Kareem another warning look. One word from Kareem at this point would bring down the man's wrath like a stack of dominoes.

"Stop it!" The unexpected order caught the ugly man unprepared. He whirled.

Jessica Carr squared her shoulders and leaned forward. Her eyes resembled two dark brown swamps. "What kind of men are you?" she cried. "We took you in and fed you. We gave you a place to sleep. Have any of you said thanks? No. It's stopped snowing. Why don't you get out of here and leave us alone?"

Deathly silence followed her outburst. The tormentor's jaw dropped. An ugly sound came from his thick throat. "Just what are you going to do about it if we don't?" he jeered. "We can kill you and be gone before anyone finds out." His horrible laugh echoed in the still room.

Some of the boys started forward. Jessica's raised hand and ringing "No!" stopped them. The inner strength that had changed her from self-pity to confident faith after tragedy, shone in her face. "You're right. You can kill us and set off a manhunt that won't stop until all of you are dead. You can even justify the lie by saying you're helping make America a better place." Jessica gripped the arms of her wheelchair and slowly stood. She took a step toward her enemy, obviously unaware she was walking. The shock of losing her father had locked her brain. Now concern for her friends unlocked it and set her legs free to move.

The others in the room stood like frozen figures in a deadly game of Statues, but Jessica wasn't finished. "There's one thing you can't do." She gazed straight into her enemy's staring eyes. "You can't stop us praying for you. Ever."

"What's going on in here?" the leader demanded from the doorway.

The sound of his voice rid the fascinated onlookers of their paralysis. Jessica glanced down. Realization that she was standing came. Amazement gave way to shock. Her weak legs, no longer sustained by crisis, crumpled. Kareem leaped, caught her just before she hit the floor, and put her back in her wheelchair.

"I asked what's going on," the leader's steely voice repeated.

A jumble of explanations poured out. Christy Gilmore's shrill voice rose above the rest: "That man was going to beat up Carlos. He said he could kill us! You won't let him hurt us, will you?" she pleaded from the shelter of Jasmine's arm.

Had God Himself prompted Christy to appeal to the white supremacist leader? The group couldn't miss seeing dull red flood his face. Or the muscle twitching in his cheek. He ignored Christy's question and commanded the seven men in camouflage, "Get your gear and wait outside." They obeyed in sullen silence.

A curious look stole across the leader's face after the

door closed. He spoke to Jessica, hurling the words like chunks of ice. "I suppose you'll thank that God of yours for bringing something good out of our being here." His thin lips twisted. "I understand that's what you Christians do."

"Yes." She met his unflinching stare. "We'll also thank him *you* were here." She didn't need to add what might have happened if he hadn't been.

The man whose name remained unknown growled low in his throat. He shot an unreadable look around the group and allowed it to linger on the Thompsons. "Your turn the other cheek stuff is stupid, but you do live what you believe." His voice chilled. "I haven't changed my mind about you. America would be better off without your kind." He turned on his boot heel and started toward the door. When he glanced back at Christy, his usual grim face showed a flicker of pain, too fleeting to be analyzed. "Good-bye, Goldilocks."

She hung onto Jasmine, eyes enormous. "Good-bye."

The door slammed behind him. After a stunned moment, Ted Hilton ran to the window, with John, Carlos, and others close behind. The intruders had already put on their skis. The group rushed to the porch and watched them disappear behind a stand of trees.

"Are they following Dave and Juli?" Shannon asked through chattering teeth.

No one answered. Screened by the trees, the men could stay together or split up and travel in any direction without being seen by those in the log house.

"They still didn't say thank you," Christy complained

when Kareem ordered them back inside. Her criticism set off an explosion of healing laughter. Yet when the group turned back to Jessica, wet eyes showed their gladness.

Christy planted herself in front of the wheelchair. "Are you going to walk some more now?" she asked.

"Jessica needs to rest," Ashley said. "She's had enough excitement. We all have!" She didn't add the thought floating in the fire-warmed cabin. The excitement wouldn't be completely over until Juli and Dave returned with help.

"Some of us could go see how the rescue crew is doing," Ted suggested.

A brief struggle showed in Kareem's face before he shook his head. "They're too far ahead of us. Besides—"

Jasmine interrupted. "We need to all stay here and dig the bus out so we'll be ready when help comes. Which it will, now that the weather is clearing." Only her tightly clenched fingers showed danger might still lurk nearby. The expressions on the faces of the men who had gone away showed it wouldn't take much for them to rebel. If they came back without their leader, anything might happen.

Juli's long-prayed-for daylight also changed her and Dave's situation from worse to impossible. Fatigue and lack of sleep had taken their toll. If the two-person rescue party hadn't been skiing downhill, they'd never have been able to keep going. Sunlight and warmer temperatures made it even harder. The frozen crust softened. In open spots, it barely held their weight.

They had passed a couple of cabins, each tightly shuttered and forlorn-looking. No help there. "If we get desperate enough we could break a window," Dave said grimly. "Only thing is, if phone lines are down, it won't help."

"I know."

They went on. Once they thought they heard the sound of a helicopter, but overlapping branches formed a canopy over the road and muffled the sound, so they couldn't be sure. Some time later, Juli heard an unfamiliar roar, foreign to the silent winter morning. She slid to a weary stop. "What is it?"

Dave's face turned the color of the world around them. "I don't know. I hope it's not the beginning of an avalanche."

"Ugh. Just what we don't need." Juli glanced up. Snowy branches bent to the ground and hid the switchbacks above them. Every horror story she'd ever heard about avalanches rushed into her tired mind. Impossible to outrun them. A maximum thirty minutes of survival time for rescue, if a person is caught and buried by rushing snow.

She thought of the band of stranded friends held captive by hate-filled men, and by the unexpected early winter storm. "We're their only hope," she whispered.

Dave didn't pretend to misunderstand. "Right." They continued on. The noise grew louder. When Dave broke into the open, he gave a yell. "Yes! It's not an avalanche, Juli, it's a snowplow!" He pointed some distance below them.

Never had anything looked more beautiful than that

heavy-duty, awkward road monster spewing snow from its gigantic blade.

"Thank God!" Juli grabbed Dave's sleeve to keep her rubber knees from giving way and depositing her in the snow.

"Shall we ski on down or wait for them here?"

Juli didn't know why she looked back the way they had come. When she did, her blood chilled. "We don't have a choice."

"What!" Dave's dark blue gaze followed her pointing finger. A moving speck that could only be someone on skis grew larger with each passing minute, obviously taking advantage of the path Dave and Juli had broken.

"Is he—it—wearing camouflage?"

"We can't wait to find out. Besides, who else could be on this mountain?" Dave's strong jaw set. "Come on. We're out of here."

Juli compared the space between them and the rapidly approaching figure with the distance to the snowplow. "We'll never make it."

"We will if we leave the road and go down there." He motioned over the bank at the edge of the road. An untouched slope connected the spot where they stood with the road a short distance in front of the plow.

A thousand objections rushed to Juli's mind. What if the snow didn't hold their weight? What if hidden dangers lay in ambush beneath the innocent-appearing whiteness? Where did the greater danger lie: below, or behind them?

She twisted her body to check on the pursuer again.

Off balance, her spaghetti-limp legs failed her. In spite of waving her arms for balance, she fell hard. Her left side smacked against a snow-covered rock at the edge of the road, and pain shot through her shoulder. She moved it to see if it worked. More pain, but it didn't seem to be broken.

"Are you okay?" Dave asked, reaching down for her.

Juli bit her lip to keep back a moan. She used her right hand to get back to her feet. "I wrenched my shoulder. You'll have to go on without me."

"You expect me to just leave you?" He looked sick.

"Yes. We knew it might come to this." She prayed for courage. "The skier won't dare hurt me with you and the men running the snowplow as witnesses. Go, Dave. For all of us."

His gaze burned into her. Without another word, he poised at the edge of the slope, flexed his knees, and pushed off.

Juli's heart jumped to her throat. She forgot the danger speeding toward her. She forgot everything except that her friend was rushing down an untried mountainside. She could see the going was tough. Twice he appeared to lose balance. Both times she cried out, "Please, God, help him." Dave recovered and sped on.

At last he reached the bottom. He clasped his hands in a victory signal and started toward the oncoming snowplow. The next moment, he cupped gloved hands around his mouth and shouted something. Distance swallowed his call. Juli couldn't understand. His pointing finger reminded her of her own danger. She heard hard breathing, then the sound of a skier plowing to a stop. A hand fell to her right shoulder. Despair filled her. So much for all her brave words about being safe because of witnesses. If the pursuer wanted to harm her, he'd have plenty of time to do so and escape before Dave and the snowplow reached her.

"Juli?" someone asked in a choked voice.

She forced herself to turn. This couldn't be happening. Not in a million years. She stared at the parka-clad man kneeling in the snow beside her. "Dad?"

"Who were you expecting, Santa Claus?" Gary Scott's laugh didn't reach the gray eyes darkened with emotion until they looked nearly black.

"No. A white supremacist." She clutched his arm to make sure he was real.

"Honey, are you delirious?" Fresh concern sprang to his face.

She shook her head. When her heart stopped thumping enough for her to talk, she said, "No. I wrenched my shoulder and couldn't go with Dave. I thought you were one of them." She knew she was babbling but couldn't seem to stop.

"Sorry. I spotted you and Dave through binoculars from the helicopter, then you skied beneath branches over the road. Didn't you see us fly over?"

She knew Dad was talking to give her time. "We thought we heard you."

"My pilot friend brought the chopper down on a level spot on a switchback above here. Lucky I had my skis. What about your shoulder?" He reached for the zipper on her parka. "When did your black and yellow ski suit turn dark green?"

Juli clenched her teeth against the pain his exploring fingers brought while making sure she hadn't dislocated her shoulder. "Too visible at night." Little by little, she told him the whole story.

When she finished, Gary Scott put on what Juli and her mother called his Washington-State-Patrol look and told her, "By the time anyone realized how bad the freak storm really was, no one could get in here." His forehead wrinkled. "Even when news came about the beating in Tacoma, and the possibility the suspects could be near here." Regret darkened his face again.

"I wish I knew what was happening at the cabin," Juli whispered.

"We'll soon find out. Can you hike up to the chopper?"

"Sure, but what about Dave?" She looked down the expanse of snow, unbroken except for twin ski tracks.

"He'll ride up on the snowplow. I'm pretty sure he recognized me. That's what the wig-wag signals were all about."

Juli nodded, saving the last of her energy for hiking. Still, Dad practically carried her the last few feet to the chopper. Tired and worried, she didn't even appreciate the thrill of riding in the Bell JetRanger. She did notice it only took minutes for them to reach the cabin. Going down through the night had felt like an eternity.

"Everything looks fine here," Dad commented when the pilot selected a level space close to the log house and set down. "Is that Shannon?" He waved at a black and yellow streak that ran to the chopper like a frightened bumblebee.

Juli felt herself coming alive. Or was she simply waking from a nightmare? Shannon's first words reassured her. "It's like I always say: Everything's swell that ends swell. The neo-Nazi's are for bein' gone, but that's not all. You'll never guess what happened, Juli! Jessica lost it when one of them was for threatenin' Carlos. She got out of her wheelchair *and walked!*"

The unexpected end to the ordeal, plus the news about Jessica, did what nothing else had been able to accomplish. Juli came unglued and burst into tears.

CHAPTER 14

The pain in Juli's shoulder lessened after Dad gave her aspirin from the Bell JetRanger's two-man survival pack. "Standard equipment," he explained. Juli and her friends marveled at the 11 by 10 by 4-inch-thick pack. It weighed only six pounds but included complete supplies and equipment: medical/first aid; food and water; signal light; emergency devices; shelter and protection (a tent and space blankets); and waterproof matches for cooking.

"I'd still rather have our log house," Ted Hilton admitted. The others quickly agreed. With the unwelcome visitors gone, their holiday spirit had returned.

The snowplow soon arrived. Dave and two broadly grinning heavy-equipment operators clambered down to loud cheers.

Others came. A Search and Rescue unit in ATVs (All Terrain Vehicles). A police helicopter, responding to the Bell JetRanger pilot's radioed message. The youth group and leaders rejoiced when they learned the

Tacoma businessman who had been beaten was no longer on the critical list.

The pilot requested that Anne Scott be informed all was well. He didn't mention Jessica's walking. Dad said this wasn't the time to tell Emily Carr.

"We know you're eager to get going," a keen-eyed officer apologized after a quick look at the church bus. Many willing hands had freed it from its prison of snow. "But we need to get your statements while things are fresh in your mind."

Gary Scott introduced himself, then said, "Would you take Juli's statement first, please? I'd like to have a doctor look at her shoulder." His gaze ranged over the others. "We'll take Jessica in the chopper and have room for one more."

Juli knew from her earlier ride that the chopper had two front seats and a three-person bench behind. "Christy may want to go, if it's all right with Dave."

"Sure. Let her finish off our adventure in style," he agreed. "Don't bother with your stuff. We'll bring it on the bus, including Jessica's wheelchair."

Fifteen minutes later, Dad lifted Jessica into the seat next to the pilot. He and Juli sat in back, with Christy in the middle like sandwich filling. The chopper lifted off. Worn-out, Juli fell asleep to the sound of whirling rotor blades and the child beside her repeating over and over how brave Jessica had been.

A short stop in Enumclaw confirmed Juli had no broken bones or dislocation. "Your shoulder needs rest," the doctor told Juli. He wrapped her arm loosely to keep it close to her body, then shook tablets into a bottle. "Take these for pain, although aspirin or acetaminophen may be all you'll need."

The rest of the flight home was hazy in Juli's mind. She drifted in and out of sleep. When they reached Bellingham, she opened heavy eyelids. Mom, Sean and Grand Riley, Emily Carr, and the Gilmores stood beside a wheelchair. Juli realized the pilot must have radioed for one while she slept.

Those gathered there showed the strain of waiting. Dad carried Jessica to the wheelchair and put her in it. Juli saw Mrs. Carr bite her lip. A lump came to Juli's throat when she said, "Nice to have you back," and kissed Jessica's cheek as if she'd simply come home from school, instead of making it a big deal.

Christy Gilmore hugged her parents, then ran to the Carrs like a pink tornado. "Scary men came to our log house and ate our food and were mean to us," she reported. "The leader made them go away, and Jessica told them to leave us alone, and oh, Mrs. Carr. . ." Christy stopped for breath. Her eyes shone like blue diamonds. "Jessica *walked*. She really, truly walked!"

Juli wanted to choke Christy, especially when Emily swayed. "Walked?" Her brown eyes so like her daughter's looked too big for her pale face. "Jessica?"

"It's true," Jessica confessed. "I got so upset at the way the intruders treated us, I guess my brain forgot to tell me my legs couldn't go. I took two whole steps." She smiled at her mother and the others. "They wouldn't let me try again until I see my specialist, but I really, truly walked, just as Christy said."

Emily Carr speechlessly hugged her daughter. Someone whispered, "Praise the Lord!" Juli met her mother's brimming gaze. An avalanche of weariness tumbled onto her. "Please, Mom, can we go home now?"

Anne brushed moisture from her eyes. "Of course. Welcome home, darling."

Hours later, Juli roused from deep sleep far more rested than she expected. She heard a light tap and called, "Come in." The door swung inward. Juli sniffed. "What smells so good?"

"Homemade chicken soup with dumplings." Her mother smiled across a full tray. "Also pickles and fruit salad. Hungry?"

"Starved. Give me a minute to wash my hands." She laughed, suddenly feeling lighthearted. "I barely remember crawling into my sleep shirt. What time is it?"

"Nine, as in P.M., not A.M., and all is well," Dad announced in a town-crier voice from the bedroom doorway. "The church bus is back and everyone safely delivered home. "Shannon is waiting in the hall. Do you want to see her?"

Juli heard a smothered giggle. She raised an eyebrow. "Should I?"

"I heard that." Her friend slid past Dad and into the room. "Mercy me, some people are certainly lazy." Her Irish eyes filled with laughter. "That's what happens when you sneak out a window in the middle of the night and go flying down a mountain road like Joan of Arc to the rescue."

Juli groaned. "Why are you wearing my parka?"

"Someone borrowed my ski suit, remember?" She dug in the pocket and held out a small slip of paper. "I can't stay. Dad's waiting in the van, but Ashley made me promise to give you this tonight. Guess what? We didn't miss any school. It's been closed for two days by the snow but we go back tomorrow. I'll see you in the morning." Shannon vanished.

Juli unfolded the paper. "I wonder why Ashley wanted me to get the message now? If it's that important, she could have called." She read the short message and silently held it out to her parents. Ashley had written:

"I asked your God to take care of you. He did. We need to talk, okay?"

"From what I know of your friend Ashley, this is a change," Dad observed.

Anne Scott's eyes glistened. "All the worry and fear of the past few days will be worthwhile if it means what it appears to mean."

Juli nodded and attacked her late, late dinner. After a warm shower, she patted Clue, took her journal notebook from her desk, and propped herself up in bed. She wrote:

Thank You so much for protecting us, God. And thank You for helping Jessica walk. I pray she will be able to keep going. Thank You I wasn't hurt badly and that Dave made it down the mountainside okay.

She stopped, nibbled her pencil, and added:

*I don't know why, but I feel this isn't really
over. Maybe it's just letdown after all the
excitement.*

Juli sighed. The capsule she had taken earlier made her
brain fuzzy. No use trying to figure out anything more
tonight. She glanced at Clue and laughed. "I didn't see
any real live relatives of yours while I was gone! It's good
to be home." She switched off her light and fell into a
deep and dreamless sleep.

In the dark hours of night, the weather changed again. A
Chinook (an Indian word meaning "warm wind") raised
the temperature dramatically. By morning, only patches
of snow remained. Gutters couldn't handle the flood of
melted snow water.

"People in the Skagit Valley will be sandbagging,"
Dad predicted at breakfast. "Especially around Mount
Vernon. The water has to go somewhere. Wonder how
close rivers are to cresting?" He excused himself to go
switch on the TV.

"Turn up the volume, will you please?" Juli called
after him.

Dad didn't reply. The sound of an announcer's voice
saying, "We interrupt our flood coverage for breaking
news. . .," brought Anne and Juli to the living room on
the run. The excited newscaster said, "The CBA,
Citizens for a Better America, has obtained a permit to

conduct a Halloween bonfire and rally in one of our parks this Friday. The CBA is suspected of being a white supremacist group."

Juli's knees gave way. She dropped to a chair. "First our variety show. Then hate group members beating people and scaring us. How can they get a permit?"

"Steady." Gary Scott squeezed her good shoulder. "The Bill of Rights guarantees the right of peaceful assembly and freedom of speech."

"How peaceful is it going to be if concerned citizens show up?" Anne cried. "One bottle rocket and there will be a riot. It has to be stopped!"

Juli had the feeling her father wasn't seeing them, although his gaze went from Mom to her. He slowly said, "I have an idea, but there's some risk."

"For whom?" Mom wanted to know. Her lips trembled.

"Juli. Me. Dave, if he wants to be in on it."

Mom's lips tightened. "I'm not having my family take any more chances."

"It could mean stopping major trouble," Dad said. "Rabble-rousing stirs emotions on both sides." Mom made a sound of protest but Dad gently put his hands on her shoulders. "You know I'd never put our daughter in real danger. You've always trusted me, Anne. Will you this time?"

A lifetime later she nodded and leaned against him.

Juli's heart raced like a jet-powered motorboat. "What's your plan, Dad?"

"I suspect your drop-in guests at the cabin won't pass up the rally. My idea is to have plainclothes officers there.

We need witnesses to positively identify the men at the cabin, especially the first five. I didn't see them; you did. The CBA will expect police, so we'll have uniformed officers visible. The group knows they can rely on noninterference if they don't break the law."

"What does Juli have to do? And Dave?" Mom demanded.

"Point out men they recognize," Dad said gruffly. "The plainclothes officers will take it from there. With God's help, there won't even be a scuffle."

Mom didn't look convinced. All she said was, "Don't wear your ski outfit or Shannon's. Cover your hair." She forced a grin. "Smear on lipstick and eye makeup, anything to serve as a disguise. If Dave goes, don't be near him. The men saw you together at Mount Rainier. Stick close to me, instead."

Juli gasped. "You're going?"

She proudly raised her head. "Why not? Do you want me to miss all the fun?"

"You two are really something," Dad told them. "Thanks."

Somehow Juli made it through the next three days at school. If the skinheads among the Hillcrest students knew anything about the mountain adventure, they kept it to themselves. Finally, Friday afternoon came. Juli felt torn between relief and excitement. It had been hard to keep her part in the rally from everyone except Dave, who quickly agreed to help. He casually told the lunch bunch he and Juli had a date that night. Shannon looked suspicious but said nothing. She'd learned long ago not to ask questions if Juli didn't confide her plans.

One bright spot was Jessica's progress. Her specialist instructed Emily to let Jessica walk a little more each day to build up muscle tone. Soon she would have no need of a wheelchair. Everyone who knew her rejoiced.

"Zero hour," a greatly disguised Juli said when they reached the park that night. She glanced at Dave. He'd donned a warm wool cap to cover his hair and turned the collar of his jacket up until it covered his chin. He squeezed Juli's hand before she joined Mom. "Be careful," he whispered, then loped after Dad.

Soon a man approached Juli and Mom. Under pretense of getting out a handkerchief, he showed his identification badge. Juli relaxed. How much danger was there in mingling with the crowd, when an officer was beside them?

The bonfire and park lights helped her in scanning faces. Juli spotted two of the self-invited guests from the log house before the rally began. She unobtrusively informed her officer and realized he must be wired. He passed on the information, barely moving his lips.

A voice coming through the sound system announced what a great honor it was to have Commandant Eisman for their speaker. A tall figure strode forward. Juli swallowed hard, remembering how frightened she had been at the top of the ski slope when she first caught sight of the man. "It's him," she breathed to the officer beside her. "The leader of the five. The other three also recognized him."

The plainclothesman quickly relayed her identification. "We want Eisman, even if we don't get all the others. We're pretty sure he was behind the bombing of the newspaper building, too," he whispered, voice barely loud enough for her to hear above the noisy crowd. "Will you be okay? I need to start moving."

Juli nodded, too excited to speak. The officer slipped away. The crowd surged forward, applauding Commandant Eisman's first ringing words, "It is time for citizens to stand up and be counted before America goes down!" Someone brushed against Juli and knocked off the baseball cap she wore to cover her hair.

Her mother's hand tightened on her arm. She turned. Mom looked so white, it frightened Juli. She mustn't faint and call attention to herself. Or to Juli, who felt unprotected without the officer and her cap. "Let's go," she whispered.

Inch by inch, they worked toward the edge of the crowd. Inch by inch they were pressed forward by the mob of people who swarmed ahead to better hear the propaganda coming from the uniformed man at the microphone. Juli's best efforts to escape proved futile. The shoving people, inflamed by Eisman's passionate speech, carried them along until they stood in daylight brightness.

Anne Scott murmured, "I'll be all right. Go, Juli. You mustn't be recognized."

"I can't just leave you!"

"You must." Juli's command to Dave from what seemed years ago echoed in her ears. So did *God can give us the strength to make hard choices.* She hadn't known how tough it would be, even though staying might put Mom in danger.

Juli ducked her head and wormed her way through the crowd. Was this how a salmon felt fighting the current on its way upstream? She pushed against people who growled. She took advantage of every bit of space to gain ground. "I'm going to be sick," she pleaded again and again. "Let me through." She wasn't lying. Her stomach felt like a giant cement mixer, and her mouth tasted gritty.

At last she made it to the outside of the tightly packed ring of observers. Relief made her light-headed. She stumbled, lurched into someone. "Watch it!" The shock of recognition made her careless for a single heartbeat. She raised her head. The man who had told Shannon that the only way to clean up a country was to kill off everyone who got in the way, stared down at her.

Had he recognized her? Juli quickly bent her head. "Sorry." She squeaked her voice to a high pitch. "I'm sick."

"Get away from me." He gave her left shoulder a shove. Pain attacked, but the push thrust her outside the range of firelight and into blessed shadows. She held back a moan and slipped behind a clump of shrubbery.

The sound of rapid steps set her running, but she couldn't escape her highly trained pursuer. "Hold it. Aren't you the girl from the mountain? The skier?"

"You hold it," Dave's hoarse voice ordered. Something dark filled his hand. "One word out of you and I'll—" He made a threatening motion.

Juli stared. Surely Dad wouldn't have given Dave a gun!

Seconds later, Gary Scott and two others appeared, both breathing hard. "We saw what happened," Dad explained. His companions made the arrest and read the man his rights. When they took the captive away, Dad laughed. "You can put down the flashlight now, Dave." Juli nearly collapsed.

An authoritative voice came through the loudspeakers just as the four reached the crowd. "Commandant Eisman, you and your men are under arrest on suspicion of. . ." A cry of protest arose. It died down when uniformed police and plainclothes officers marched in. "Go home," the officer in charge commanded.

The sullen crowd scattered, still muttering. "Wait for me here," Gary Scott told Dave and Juli. "I'll go get Anne." He disappeared into the thinning group.

"They're bringing Eisman," Dave whispered.

Juli gulped. Seeing even those who *deserved* their handcuffs wasn't pleasant.

She couldn't help feeling things would have been far worse at the cabin if there had been a different commandant. Her heart beat faster. Eisman walked so tall, so proudly: a leader who had chosen the wrong path. Why had he risked capture by speaking tonight? He was too smart not to realize the danger. Perhaps he felt being imprisoned would call attention to his cause. Fanatical persons often became martyrs in order to gain sympathy.

The police brought Eisman within a few feet of Dave

and Juli. He glanced at the disguised girl without recognition, but halted in front of the tall boy. "Can the girl in the wheelchair still walk?"

"Yes." Dave's glad reply rang in the night air.

"So miracles never cease, at least for some people." His face twisted. Juli saw in the flickering light the same pain she'd noticed at the log house. The officers led him away, but Eisman called back, "Take care of Goldilocks."

"What does he mean by that?" Juli asked.

Dave shook his head. "I don't know. Jasmine said when he left the cabin with his men, he called Christy Goldilocks and told her good-bye. Maybe she reminds him of someone. I hate unfinished stories, but I have a feeling this part of our latest mystery will remain unsolved."

The next afternoon, Juli repeated Dave's comment to Shannon. The girls had curled up on the twin beds in Juli's sunny room for a long-delayed talk.

Her Irish friend said, "I'm like Dave. I don't like stories with loose ends. I want everything tied up with neat little bows." She sighed. "Too bad life isn't like that. By the way, is Ashley's note a secret?"

"Not from you, but keep it to yourself." Juli felt her eyes sting. "She said she asked 'my' God to take care of me. He did and she says we need to talk."

Shannon looked awed. "Mercy me, what a long way for her to come!"

"That's what Dad and Mom said. At least she's starting to believe there is a God. Seeing what happened with

Jessica may strengthen that belief."

Shannon yawned. "I hope so. Right now, it's nice to have a piece of quiet."

"Don't you mean peace *and* quiet?" Juli teased.

Shannon shook her dark head until her bangs bounced. "No! We're for needin' an enormous piece of quiet before our next adventure."

Juli laughed. "Bad as I hate to admit it, I couldn't agree more!"

Kid Stuff
Fun-filled Activity Books
for ages 7-12

Bible Questions and Answers for Kids
Collection #1 and #2

Brain-teasing questions and answers from the Bible are sure to satisfy the curiosity of any kid. And fun illustrations combined with Bible trivia make for great entertainment and learning! Trade paper; 8 ½" x 11" $2.97 each.

Bible Crosswords for Kids
Collection #1 and #2

Two great collections of Bible-based crossword puzzles are sure to challenge kids ages seven to twelve. Hours of enjoyment and Bible learning are combined into these terrific activity books. Trade paper; 8 ½" x 11" $2.97 each.

The Kid's Book of Awesome Bible Activities
Collection #1 and #2

These fun-filled, Bible-based activity books include challenging word searches, puzzles, hidden pictures, and more! Bible learning becomes fun and meaningful with *The Kid's Book of Awesome Bible Activities.* Trade paper; 8 ½" x 11" $2.97 each.
